ACCLAIM FOR

TO MARRY AN ENGLISH LORD

"Go West, dear readers! I literally could not put this book down and was up much of the night delighting in the story world and watching the characters grow, both in their faith and in their love for one another. You'll be encouraged in your faith, too, as you adventure with Viscount Willowthorpe to an Idaho ranch where he encounters businesswoman and ranch co-owner Jocelyn Overstreet, a woman like none he has ever met."
– Stephanie Grace Whitson, author of *Love at First Light*

"An absolute gem of a story! If you're craving romance set against the vast beauty of the untamed west, then look no further. Filled with witty repartee and heartfelt emotion, Robin Lee Hatcher's second installment in The British Are Coming series is guaranteed to please!"
— Tamera Alexande*r, USA Today* Bestselling author of *A Million Little Choices* and *Colors of Truth*

"Master storyteller Robin Lee Hatcher has penned an engaging sweet romance, laced with inspiration and a vivid depiction of our Wild West. The way the two main characters slowly discover their forbidden love and lean on God for guidance plucks at the heartstrings. The setting of a cattle ranch situated in an untamed landscape of rolling hills and mountains steal one's breath. All the while, an unobtrusive portrayal of the bittersweet changing lifestyle of the American cowboy more than enchanted this avid history aficionada."

— Linda Windsor, author of Irish and Scottish historical romance collections

---

"There is a reason Robin Lee Hatcher has a large and loving following. Her love of the Lord combines with compassion and a deep understanding of humanity. In *To Marry an English Lord*, Sebastian and Jocelyn and even minor characters soon transcend into realistic people, people I know, people like me. Thanks to her lovely writing style and authentic sense of time and place, it's a delight to be drawn into the worlds Robin creates, where God's love and eternal presence abound."

— Dandi Daley Mackall, author of *Women Who Followed Jesus: 40 Devotions on the Journey to Easter*

"Get ready for sparks and a wild ride when an English lord and an East Coast businesswoman meet on a ranch in the wild west. Robin Lee Hatcher can't be beat."

— Hannah Alexander, author of *One Strong Man*

"I have always loved Robin Lee Hatcher's contemporary romance novels, but I was excited to read *To Marry an English Lord*, a historical set in the American West, which features the story of Jocelyn Overstreet, a feisty American woman who is strong and independent, and the dashing Sebastian Whitcombe, Viscount Willowthorpe, who comes to Eden's Gate Ranch in Idaho to experience the cowboy ways and to figure out his future. These two have instant chemistry and are soon in love, but Sebastian's ornery father and the constant problems on the ranch keep them apart. This is a sweet story that will keep readers enthralled until the beautiful end."

— Lenora Worth, author of *Disappearance in Pinecraft*

"To Marry an English Lord is the perfect fictional getaway and romantic escape. Idaho provides the perfect rugged backdrop for swoon-worthy Sebastian to shed his proper English ways and question his lineage when he meets the beautiful, but feisty Jocelyn Overstreet. All of the characters jumped off the page, and I wanted to step back in time with them. In Hatcher's talented hands, this romance will keep you up late and stay with you long after you close the book. Another five star read by Robin Lee Hatcher."

— Kristin Billerbeck, award-winning author of *The View from Above*

cup of hot tea and a plush throw, and curl up to savor *To Enchant a Lady's Heart,* the delightful novella launching Robin Lee Hatcher's newest series, The British are Coming!"

— Tamera Alexander, *USA Today* bestselling author of *Colors of Truth*

"Such a sweet, engaging story! I fell in love with spunky Amanda, goodhearted Adam, and dear Eliza who longed to be seen for herself and not for what her father's wealth could bring to the table. I enjoyed every minute of my time at Hooke Manor and look forward to a return visit in Sebastian's story."

— Kim Vogel Sawyer, bestselling author of *Still My Forever*

To Marry An English Lord

THE BRITISH ARE COMING
BOOK TWO

ROBIN LEE HATCHER

Paperback ISBN: 978-1-962005-02-9
eBook ISBN: 978-1-962005-01-2

Library of Congress Control Number: 2023924101

Published by RobinSong, Inc.
Meridian, Idaho

Dedicated to the One who makes life a great adventure.

Chapter One

Eden's Gate Ranch, Idaho
May 21, 1895

S ebastian Whitcombe, Viscount Willowthorpe, reined in the hired gelding at the top of the rise and waited for the coach carrying his sister, Amanda, and his artist friend, Roger Bernhardt, to catch up to him.

Before the vehicle stopped, his sister's head poked out the open window. "What is it? Are there buffalo?"

"No buffalo, Amanda. But we are almost to our destination." He dismounted, then pointed into the distance. "Eden's Gate Ranch. Our home for the coming year."

The coach door opened, and Roger stepped to the ground, then turned and helped Amanda do the same. Together, the three took in the view. On the opposite side of a deep, verdant valley sat a house and numerous outbuildings. The house looked to be large by most standards, though not when compared to Hooke Manor, seat of the earls of Hooke for more than two centuries.

"Look at that sky," Roger said. "Look at those mountains. Breathtaking."

Sebastian grinned. If Roger had his way, he would pull out canvas and paints and immediately get to work capturing the spectacular mountain peaks that rose off to their right on the eastern side of the ranch.

"Could we enjoy the view later?" Amanda asked, a touch of petulance in her voice. "I'm famished, and it's been a long day."

Sebastian had to agree with her. They were all tired and hungry—and that had to include the driver perched atop the coach. After a week-long train trip across the country, the travelers had spent last night in a rustic hotel in Pocatello, Idaho, a city of about ten thousand people. They'd risen early this morning to travel north to the Overstreet ranch, Amanda and Roger in a hired rig—along with many trunks and suitcases—and Sebastian on horseback.

Ignoring Amanda, Roger turned in a slow circle, taking in the view from all directions. "How long has it been since you've seen this friend of yours?"

"About seven or eight years. William was supposed to take over the family shipping business in New York City. But when the time came to take the reins from his father, he turned his back on shipping and the big city and moved to this cattle ranch. It was established by his mother's family, I understand, back during the time gold was discovered throughout this region. From what I can tell by his letters, he never regretted his decision."

"Is he the reason you were so set on this trip?"

Sebastian smiled. "Partly. When we were at school together, he had a way of describing this valley, this whole country, that made me eager to see it for myself. I knew America was large, of course, but I wasn't prepared for the vastness of it. Or of its ever-changing beauty."

Roger murmured agreement before helping Amanda back into the coach. After remounting the gelding, Sebastian looked down on the valley in the shadow of the rugged Rocky Mountains. The next year would be amazing. He had no doubt about it.

As they set off at a brisk pace, Sebastian frowned, remembering what would follow his year in America— he would return to England, marry a girl who met with his father's approval, and do his duty to provide an heir. As the earl liked to remind him, Sebastian wasn't getting any younger. At thirty-two, it was time for him to settle down and learn to run Hooke Manor and the other Whitcombe estates.

"And I won't live forever," his father had never failed to add.

Maybe not forever, but judging by Edward Whitcombe's robust health, for a good many more years to come. So why the need for Sebastian to marry?

He gave himself a mental shake. He would not dwell on that now. He was in America, and he meant to enjoy this adventure to the full.

Half an hour later, the Whitcombe party arrived at their destination. The exterior of the large ranch house was made of fieldstone in gray, white, and gold. L-shaped, it had three stories and an abundance of windows. They would hardly be roughing it while staying here.

Sebastian dismounted and looped the reins around a post. He was about to turn to the coach when the front door opened and a portly woman in a black dress stepped onto the veranda, frowning, as if their arrival displeased her.

"Good day, madam," he said. "I am Sebastian Whitcombe. William's friend from Eton. I believe you are expecting us."

"And I am Mrs. Adler, Mr. Overstreet's housekeeper."

Sebastian glanced at the land beyond the corrals, fences, and outbuildings. It was dotted with brown cattle, both near and into the distance. Just as William had described it. Looking back at the housekeeper, he asked, "Is Mr. Overstreet around?"

"Yes, sir. But he's not able to greet you himself. There's been an accident."

"An accident?" His gaze shot back to the woman. "Is it serious?"

"Serious enough." She drew herself up, her expression even more disapproving. "And because of you lot, he's had himself moved out of his room."

"May I see him?"

"No, you may not. Dr. Grant says he's not to be disturbed."

4

"But—"

"Come with me." The housekeeper's words were more command than invitation. "Might as well get you all settled."

As THE TEAM of horses pulled the rented coach closer to Eden's Gate, Jocelyn Overstreet thanked God the journey was nearly over. She'd been lucky to have found an available coach and driver to hire. Apparently another party had left the Pocatello livery in a newer coach half an hour or so before she'd arrived.

"This is the only rig I got left," the proprietor had said. "It's not as comfortable, but it'll get you there. And the team's dependable."

She closed her eyes, willing away the headache that had tortured her ever since she'd received the telegram from Mrs. Adler a week ago.

William in accident. Serious. Come quickly.

A serious accident. That's all she'd been told. But it had been enough to cause her to drop everything and catch the next available train out of New York City.

Six years had passed since Jocelyn's last trip to Idaho. She'd been twenty-three at the time and already had been in charge of Overstreet Shipping for two years. The demands of the business made it difficult to leave New York, despite her desire to return to the ranch they'd inherited from their mother, despite her desire to spend time with her beloved older brother. Now, at last, she was here again.

She opened her eyes and looked out the coach window at the passing terrain—pale grasses waving in a breeze, tall pines, whispering aspens, and gnarly cottonwoods breaking the rolling landscape, the Teton Range resplendent in its rocky majesty. How had she let so much time go by since she was last here? She loved this country. She loved the ranch. She loved riding horses and herding cattle. She loved sitting by the fire with William and recalling stories from their childhood before he'd been sent to England for his schooling. She loved the changing seasons, seasons that were distinct, seasons that could be harsh even while beautiful.

Leaning back again, Jocelyn closed her eyes and sent up a quick prayer for her brother. Whatever had happened to him, no matter how serious, she had to trust God with the outcome. Trust God . . . and Mrs. Adler. That woman would fight tooth and nail to make sure William was okay. He'd always been the housekeeper's favorite.

Even her headache couldn't keep her from smiling over that thought.

The coach slowed as it began a slow descent into the valley. She sat forward a second time, but she already knew what she would see beyond the coach window. While she had lived most of her life in the East and knew the streets of Manhattan and the docks along the Hudson as well as she knew her own name, it was here in this Idaho valley where her heart came alive. If she leaned out the window, she would be able to see the large stone house, the cattle on the range, the horses in the corrals. She resisted the urge. She didn't need to appear any more bedraggled than she already felt.

When the coach arrived at last, she didn't wait for the driver to get down from his perch and open the door for her. She opened it herself—even as the vehicle rocked back and forth—and jumped to the ground.

Lifting the skirt of her travel dress, she ran to open the front door of the stone house. "Billy! Mrs. Adler!"

Receiving no reply, she hurried toward the stairs. As she rounded a corner, she ran into a broad chest.

"By heaven!" The stranger caught her by the shoulders, steadying her.

She stepped back, out of his reach. He was a tall man, and by his dress she knew he wasn't one of her brother's cowboys.

"May I be of some assistance to you?" he asked.

She chose not to answer. Instead, she took another step back and demanded, "Who are you? What are you doing in my brother's house?"

"I am Sebastian Whitcombe, madam. I live here." He cocked an imperious brow. "And who, might I ask, are you?"

Jocelyn took one more step back.

"Miss Joss? Is that you?"

Relief flooded through her at the sound of the housekeeper speaking her nickname, and she whirled about to face the woman. "Mrs. Adler. I came as soon as I received the telegram." She cast a glance over her shoulder at the stranger, then returned her eyes to the older woman. "Where is Billy?"

"He's in the guest cottage, miss. He'll be glad to see you."

The guest cottage? Why was her brother in the guest cottage? And who was this man who claimed to live here?

Chapter Two

Sebastian watched Mrs. Adler take the younger woman by the arm.

"Come with me, Miss Joss. I'll take you to Mr. William."

A moment later, Sebastian stared at the closed front door. "Miss Joss," he whispered. So that fiery creature with the wild curls and sparking hazel eyes was William's younger sister. She wasn't quite what he'd imagined, but back when William had spoken of her she'd been a girl. And now she was a woman—and a beautiful one at that.

Aloud, he added, "A woman who resents my presence, apparently."

How had it happened that he was on the wrong side of both the housekeeper and Jocelyn Overstreet? Sebastian was sought after by many in society. For heaven's sake, he'd come to America to get away from the matchmaking mothers—and a few fathers—who wanted him for a son-in-law.

After crossing the large parlor, he looked out the window in time to see Mrs. Adler and Jocelyn disappear into a smaller stone building. The guest cottage, he presumed, where William had taken up residence. But why had his friend thought that necessary? If Sebastian had had a little more time after arriving and being shown about the house, he would have convinced Mrs. Adler to take him to see William, whether she liked it or not. Whether she liked *him* or not. But there hadn't been time. Not before William's sister had barreled into his chest.

"Sebastian!" Amanda called from upstairs. "You must come see your bedchamber. There is an enormous bear rug on the floor. I've never seen anything like it before."

He nodded, as if his sister could see him, but his attention remained on the guest cottage.

"Sebastian! Do come see it."

With a sigh, he turned and walked to the staircase. It wasn't grand by the standards of Hooke Manor, but it was impressive, nonetheless. The handrail was fashioned of uncut wood stripped free of bark, polished, and varnished. The steps themselves were deep, made for a man wearing boots, not a woman in dainty dancing shoes. He grinned. He loved America.

"Sebastian, you won't believe it." Amanda poked her head through an open doorway. "There's a water closet with a flush toilet. Out here. In the wilderness. I never expected that." She joined him in the hallway, hooked her arm through his, and drew him toward a room at the end of the hall. "You get the largest bedchamber, of course. Roger already brought your trunks up while you were trying to converse with the housekeeper. What did you learn?"

"The woman wasn't very talkative. I still don't know anything of importance."

Amanda laughed. "She is never going to forgive us for invading the Overstreet home."

"We were invited. Multiple times. And we compensated the owner. More than he asked, I should add. It's our right to be here, and I refuse to feel guilty about it."

"I don't believe Mrs. Adler sees it as our right, no matter how much rent you pay."

"Then I shall have to win her over with my charms."

"Whoever said you were charming?"

He feigned offense, causing Amanda to laugh again.

"*I* certainly never called you charming, Whitcombe." Roger appeared in a bedchamber doorway. "I'm feeling rather peckish. Are we to see to our own meals?"

"Sorry." Sebastian moved toward his friend. "Mrs. Adler showed me the kitchen, but I failed to ask what time we would eat or where to find the cook. In the excitement of our arrival, I forgot how hungry we all are. But I've remembered now. Let's have a look."

The three of them headed downstairs, then followed a hallway to the back of the house.

In the homes where Sebastian resided or visited, food appeared at an appointed time. Or, at the very least, at the ring of a bell. He saw no bells in this house. However, between him, his sister, and his friend, they would surely be able to find something to satisfy their hunger.

The Eden's Gate kitchen looked quite large. It might well be larger than the one at Hooke Manor. Perhaps it was the absence of a cook and other servants bustling about making it look this way. After all, he'd only seen the kitchen when he was a boy, sneaking out of the house to join his half-brother Adam on a late-night ride. He couldn't be sure his memories were accurate.

A door beyond a small entry hall opened, letting more daylight spill into the kitchen. A few moments later, a grizzled older man appeared in the opening. "Well, how do." He grinned. "You must be that fancy count who's come to stay."

"Viscount," Sebastian corrected, then wished he'd stayed silent. Titles meant nothing in America. At least not in the American West. He cleared his throat before offering his hand. "I'm Sebastian Whitcombe."

"Mighty fancy name you got there. The boys call me Chuck. Kind of a joke. In my younger days, I drove the chuck wagon on cattle drives. Real name's Kincaid. Stewart Kincaid. But you're welcome to call me Chuck too, if you've a mind to."

Sebastian nodded, unsure how to respond to that wealth of information.

"I'm here to rustle you up some grub," Chuck said.

Rustle? Grub? What on earth did that mean?

Speaking slowly—as if he thought Sebastian none too bright—the older man added, "I'm the cook here on Eden's Gate."

"By heaven, that's good news," Roger all but shouted. "We're all frightfully hungry."

Chuck arched an eyebrow as he crossed the room and took a white apron from a hook on the wall. "You folks give me a short while. I'll let you know when chow's ready for you."

Chow? Was that another word for the midday meal? Sebastian had believed Americans spoke the King's English. William did, as he recalled. Then again, William had spent most of his school years in England.

He looked down the hallway toward the salon or the drawing room or whatever it was called. Should they wait there until they were summoned by the cook? No, he felt too restless for that.

"Shall we explore the ranch?" he asked his friend and sister.

Amanda gave a small shake of her head. "I would rather rest. I'll be in my room."

"Roger?"

"I'll beg off. I want to put my paint box in order and organize the rest of my supplies. I haven't looked through the trunk since I packed it before leaving England. I want to make sure there is nothing I need to replace."

Sebastian gave a nod.

Chuck said, "I'll ring the dinner bell when lunch is ready." He chuckled. "And don't you worry none. You'll know it when you hear it."

Jocelyn leaned forward on the straight-backed chair next to her brother's bed. "You look dreadful, Billy."

"You already said that," William replied, eyes closed. "Three times." His face was ashen and dark circles underscored his eyes. Stubble darkened his jaw, making him look older than his thirty-two years.

She looked around the bedroom. A third the size of the master bedroom in the main house, it was tidy but plain. No paintings hung on the walls, and there was only one window to let in sunlight. Her gaze returned to her brother. "When did you see the doctor last?"

"Dr. Grant came to the ranch yesterday. Says I am out of danger from infection." He winced, unable to hide his pain. "Mrs. Adler's made sure I'm well taken care of." He glanced toward the door where the housekeeper stood, her hands folded over her apron.

Jocelyn relaxed slightly—and tried not to imagine the moment the buffalo had gored her brother in the leg.

As if reading her mind, William said, "It was my own fault, Jocelyn. I should have shot it rather than try to run it away from the cattle. But there're so few buffalo left, I couldn't do it. Seemed wrong to shoot it. At least it didn't kill my horse. It only got me."

"Billy, we have other horses." She leaned toward him again. "We only have one you."

"Amen to that," Mrs. Adler said, ending with an *harrumph* for good measure.

"But why are you staying in the guest house? You'd be more comfortable in your own room, wouldn't you?"

"Maybe. But I was planning to move out here anyway."

"Why?"

"I guess Mrs. Adler didn't tell you." He looked toward the housekeeper who shook her head. "Not surprised." His gaze returned to Jocelyn. "I've got a friend who's coming from England. We were in school together. His name is Sebastian. Sebastian Whitcombe, Viscount Willowthorpe. In fact, he should arrive—"

"That man in the house is a friend of yours?"

William went silent a moment. Then he sat up a little straighter. "Is Sebastian here? Why didn't anyone tell me?"

Mrs. Adler answered, "He and the others arrived not long before Miss Joss. I didn't have time to tell you."

"You could've told me when you brought Jocelyn over."

"I could've," the housekeeper retorted, "but you're not supposed to have visitors. Remember what the doctor said."

"But you brought Jocelyn."

"She's no visitor. She's family."

William sank against the pillows at his back, his burst of energy over. He rolled his head to the side to look at Jocelyn again. "Sebastian's a good friend. A very good friend. We've stayed in touch ever since I returned to America. I invited him to come stay at the ranch. Asked him every time I wrote. Finally, he took me up on the offer. Insisted on paying rent, too. His sister and a friend came with him."

"Paid rent?"

"I want to see him. I should have been there to welcome him."

She moved her hand from his wrist to his upper arm. "You're not getting out of this bed until the doctor says you can."

He nodded and closed his eyes. "Then you'll have to make them feel welcome. I want them here . . . Need them here."

Silence settled over the bedroom.

Whispering, Mrs. Adler said, "I'll go back to the main house. Barely had time to show Mr. Whitcombe the downstairs before you turned up. Heaven knows what they might be gettin' into on their own. Lord this and lady that. Takin' over the house. As if we need them and their hoity-toity ways around Eden's Gate. I don't care how much Mr. William wanted them to come."

Jocelyn twisted on the chair to look at the house-keeper. "How long do they plan to stay?"

"A year."

Jocelyn drew back. "Good heavens! A year?"

After Mrs. Adler left, Jocelyn faced the bed again. Even in sleep, William's face revealed the pain he was in. And no wonder, doing battle with a buffalo. As a girl, she'd seen one walk up to the corral, jump the fence, gore a horse, killing it, then depart the way it had come, blood dripping from its horns.

Drawing a deep breath, she rose and went to the window. The barnyard was quiet at this time of day, all the men out doing their ranch work. A dog slept near the front porch, enjoying the warmth of the sun against the hard-packed earth. A couple of horses stood near a water trough, eyes closed and tails still.

The scene was tranquil. Her thoughts were not.

That man, Sebastian Whitcombe, had paid William rent, with plans to stay for the next year. Did a friend pay rent when he came for a visit? Even a long one. And why had her brother said he *needed* them here? That seemed an odd comment. Very odd, indeed.

While her brother's letters had come regularly, he never shared much of substance. News of the weather. Updates on the cowboys. Some rare gossip about the folks in Gibeon, the town that lay about an hour west of the ranch. But not much else. Little about himself. Nothing about his feelings. And he'd certainly never mentioned taking rent money and turning over the house to some strangers from England.

She glanced at the bed and her sleeping brother. "I suppose I need to welcome your guests."

William didn't stir.

She crossed the room to check her reflection. It told her she looked like someone who'd traveled by train for days, followed by too many hours in a coach. But what could she do about it now? With a sigh, she turned from the mirror and left the guest cottage.

Chapter Three

As Jocelyn walked toward the main house, she heard the clang of the dinner bell. Immediately her mouth watered, and she realized she was more than ready to eat. If Chuck was serving lunch, she meant to be at the table, no matter what William's guests thought about it.

Sebastian Whitcombe came around the corner of the house before Jocelyn reached the front door. At the sight of him, her footsteps faltered, and she stopped to watch his approach. He was a handsome man with thick, dark hair. But something about him made her bristle. Why? Was it merely because his presence on the ranch had surprised her or was it something else?

Seeing her, he also stopped. "Miss Overstreet. I'm sorry we weren't properly introduced earlier."

"And I'm sorry I wasn't expecting you, Mr. Whitcombe." She hesitated. "Or do you prefer I call you Lord Whitcombe?"

The corners of his mouth twitched, as if he resisted

a smile. "I prefer to leave formal titles of address back in England. Mr. Whitcombe will suit me well for the duration."

Despite herself, she liked him for that answer.

His expression turned serious. "May I ask, how is William? Your housekeeper told me nothing and refused to let me see him when I asked."

"He's in considerable pain, but I'm told he should make a full recovery."

"What happened?"

She shook her head. "I don't know many details. He tried to drive a buffalo away from some cattle, and it gored him in the leg. It's a deep wound, but thankfully no bones were broken. The doctor believes he is free of infection."

"That sounds serious. From what I've been told about the American bison, William could have been killed."

"You were told correctly. We rarely see buffalo on Eden's Gate. They've been hunted almost to extinction. But there are a few small herds still living in and near the national park. Every so often, one works its way down to this valley. The cowboys try to avoid them as they are unpredictable beasts." The clang of the bell sounded again, and Jocelyn turned toward the door. "We'd better not keep Chuck waiting. He never rings more than twice." She assumed that was still true, despite the passing of six years since her last visit to the ranch.

Sebastian hurried to open the door for her. She acknowledged his polite gesture with a nod as she entered the house. But that didn't mean she was glad to have him on Eden's Gate. She would rather have her girlhood home to herself. She would rather see to her brother in his own bedroom instead of the guest house. Was she supposed to play hostess or was she suddenly an unwelcome guest in the Overstreet home?

When Jocelyn and Sebastian entered the dining room, she saw Mrs. Adler standing at attention near the sideboard, looking as if she was there to guard the china and silverware. Closer to the table were the rest of Sebastian's party. William had said they were Sebastian's sister and a friend, but no names had been mentioned. Should she introduce herself?

As if sensing Jocelyn's uncertainty, Sebastian said, "Amanda, Roger, may I introduce William's sister, Miss Jocelyn Overstreet. Miss Overstreet, this is my sister, Lady Amanda Whitcombe, and our friend, Mr. Roger Bernhardt."

Amanda Whitcombe looked to be in her early twenties with the same chocolate brown eyes, dark hair, and striking good looks as her brother. But where he was tall and broad-shouldered, she was petite and slight of build. Roger Bernhardt, with his fair hair and blue eyes, seemed pale in comparison to the siblings, although his smile was warm.

Amanda rounded the table and reached for Jocelyn's hand. "How very happy I am to meet you, Miss Overstreet. I weary of these two men for company. Can you imagine what it was like for me, always being with them on the ship, then on the train, and finally in the coach that brought us to this ranch? I have longed for female companionship. Our brothers are good friends. I hope we will become good friends, too."

Jocelyn had spent most of her adult life around men. Was that something to be weary of? Men on the docks. Men in the boardroom. Male attorneys. Male bankers. A male secretary to help her with the day-to-day running of Overstreet Shipping. Her female acquaintances in New York were mostly the wives of the men she worked with, and those women—more often than not—seemed suspicious of an unwed female in charge of a company. Not a close friend among them.

Amanda squeezed her hand, drawing Jocelyn's attention back to her. "Do call me Amanda."

She drew a breath and released it. "And you must call me Jocelyn."

"I will." Amanda's smile broadened and her eyes seemed to twinkle with merriment. "My father would not approve of the informality, of course." She leaned closer to Jocelyn and lowered her voice. "But thankfully, Father is not here."

"Amanda," Sebastian said in a low but firm voice.

His sister sighed. "Don't act high and mighty with me, Sebastian. You have enjoyed your freedom every bit as much as I have." She gave a slight toss of her head before returning to the opposite side of the table.

Mrs. Adler stepped away from the sideboard and close to the chair that had always been Jocelyn's. "You'd best all be seated before the food gets cold."

As Jocelyn took her seat, she observed Sebastian taking silent cues from the redoubtable Mrs. Adler. The party of guests all sat, leaving William's chair empty.

The care taken by Sebastian to make certain no one sat where they shouldn't made Jocelyn's attitude toward him soften a little more.

OVER THE YEARS, Sebastian had watched his sister grow gracefully into the role of hostess at the manor. She excelled at drawing people into conversation, no matter the setting, no matter their class.

"Have you been away from Eden's Gate for long?" Amanda asked Jocelyn the moment everyone was settled.

"Away?" Jocelyn seemed to consider, then shook her head. "Not in the way you mean. My home is in New York City. Mrs. Adler sent for me after Billy was injured."

"You live alone in New York?" Amanda's eyes widened. "I can't imagine being alone in such a big city."

Sebastian had thought the same thing.

The housekeeper set a large platter of sliced beef in the center of the table. "Where else would Miss Joss live as long as she's in charge of the family's shipping business? The office is in New York, so there she's gotta be."

Sebastian waited for a reprimand from Jocelyn Overstreet. He'd never known a servant to interrupt a conversation at the dining table in such a way. But no reprimand came. Almost as if the interruption by the housekeeper wasn't deemed unusual at all.

"You run a business? A shipping business?" Amanda's eyes widened.

If Jocelyn was insulted by the shock in his sister's expression, she didn't show it. "I do. I am the director of Overstreet Shipping. William and I own the company together, but I manage it."

Amanda turned in Sebastian's direction. "Father would be . . . Well, he would find it beyond the pale. Wouldn't he?"

Yes, their father would find it unthinkable. But Sebastian thought it intriguing. Almost as intriguing as he found William's sister. "How long have you been in charge of the company, Miss Overstreet?"

"Since my father's death. Eight years now. But I worked with him for a number of years before that."

"I always expected—" He broke off abruptly, afraid he would say the wrong thing.

"That Billy would take the helm?" she finished for him.

He nodded.

"My brother hated the city, and he disliked the business."

Sebastian nodded. William had frequently complained about both while they were in school. "Now that you mention it, I remember. And he never made a secret of how much he hated sailing back and forth between America and England. He didn't care for the sea at all. After he left England for good, he never said anything in his letters about working with your father. Next thing I knew, he wrote to me from this ranch and insisted I come stay with him. He swore he would turn me into one of the cowboys, and he had plenty to say about the beauty of this valley and the mountains that surround it."

A smile flitted across Jocelyn's mouth. It was a generous, rosy-hued mouth. Quite fetching with the corners curved upward.

His own mouth suddenly dry, he swallowed and looked at the food on the table before him. There were no footmen carrying platters and bowls to each person at the table. He knew they would each serve themselves and pass the platters around the table, and he waited for a signal from their hostess—wasn't Jocelyn their hostess? —that it was time to begin.

Glancing her way, he saw her bow her head. He did the same. Her thanks to God for the food on the table was soft and brief. After her amen, she looked at him again and gave a nod, then lifted the platter closest to her plate.

After everyone had passed the serving bowls and filled their own plates, Sebastian said, "Miss Overstreet, may I ask why William is staying in the guest cottage?"

Her gold-flecked eyes widened. "Because you rented the house, of course."

"What? But it's a large house. There are plenty of bedrooms. It was never my intention for William to live elsewhere during our stay. He should be in his own room. It will certainly be easier for you and Mrs. Adler to care for him if he's in the main house. Is that not true?"

"Yes, it would be much easier, Mr. Whitcombe."

Sebastian looked at each person around the table.

"It never occurred to me he would think it necessary to move out."

"I'll speak to him about it, but I'm not sure he will agree." She lifted her knife and fork and cut the meat on her plate in a bite-size piece.

"If you'll permit me to join you, I am quite certain I can change his mind."

She glanced up again, ignoring the food on her fork. "Don't be so sure. You haven't seen each other in years, and he seemed quite determined about the arrangements."

Amanda leaned forward. "When he sets his mind to it, Sebastian is ever so persuasive, especially among his friends."

Jocelyn's gaze lowered. "Then I hope his luck will hold with Billy. My brother can be equally stubborn."

Sebastian loved nothing if not a challenge. He suppressed a smile, turning his attention to the food before him. First, he would show Miss Overstreet he could persuade William to reside in the house with his paying guests. And then he would make her fond of him. By heaven, he would.

Chapter Four

Sebastian was successful in convincing William to move back into his own bedchamber in the main house—the large room with the bear rug Amanda had exclaimed over on the day they arrived. But during his first week in Idaho, Sebastian was less successful in making William's sister think better of him, mostly because she was rarely in his company. She took her meals with her brother in his bedchamber at the far end of one wing of the house and must have spent most of the rest of her time there as well. She had become a ghost within the house, a presence he watched for but rarely caught a glimpse of.

However, he didn't dwell on his seeming failure. He was too interested in the cattle operation, in the cowboys who worked the ranch, in the vastness of the valley and the ranch itself—all nine-thousand-plus acres of it—as well as in the magnificent mountains to the southeast of Eden's Gate.

"Breathtaking," Roger had dubbed the Tetons on

their arrival. And they were, particularly at sunset when the light hit them just right, painting them an unexpected vermilion.

Now, as Sebastian and Roger stood near a wooden fence, staring toward the rugged mountain range, Roger said, "I will never be able to capture on canvas the way they look in real life. But I mean to try. And try. And try."

Sebastian leaned his forearms on the top rail. "While you try to capture those mountains on canvas, I'm eager to ride along with the men who work here. Maybe get up close to those same mountains."

"What will the earl have to say if you return home a real cowboy?" Roger laughed. "I shudder to think."

"I didn't travel all this way to go on living as I did in England."

"Of course not."

"I want to experience what it's like to work on a cattle ranch, day in and day out."

"And I hope that's what you do."

"You should plan to come along with us."

Roger laughed softly. "If you wanted someone to ride with you, you should have brought Adam to America instead of me."

Sebastian nodded, imagining his older half-brother on this ranch. Adam would have loved the experience, no doubt. But he now managed the entire Hooke Manor estate as well as overseeing the Whitcombe stables. And then there was the matter of Adam's new bride. Eliza wouldn't have approved any plan that would take her husband away for a year.

A cool breeze caused the long grass in the nearby paddock to wave and dance, and shadows began to creep up the base of the mountain range.

Roger broke the lengthy silence. "Life is going to be quite different when we return to England."

"Indeed."

Sebastian envisioned the weeks of intimate soirees and elaborate balls he would be forced to attend as he sought a wife. He'd made a promise to his father that he would be engaged within a year after his return to England, but thinking of it left a bad taste in his mouth. It wasn't because he was against marriage. His parents had been uncommonly contented, despite the union being arranged for them. But finding the right woman? That wouldn't be easy. He'd met too many simpering, vacuous females over the years. The last thing he wanted was to be married to a woman who couldn't hold his interest, who didn't have a single unique thought in her head.

Jocelyn Overstreet's image drifted into his thoughts. She was anything but simpering or vacuous. She ran a successful business—a man's business in a man's world —and to do so took wit and intelligence, not to mention a healthy dose of fortitude.

But what would the Earl of Hooke think of her?

He laughed, drawing Roger's gaze.

"What?" his friend asked.

Sebastian shook his head. "Nothing. I was thinking about my father."

"And *that* made you laugh?"

"Father doesn't understand my fascination with this

country." He lowered his voice, mimicking the earl. "Zounds! It was not that long ago we were fighting a war with them. Uncivilized, uncouth lot."

Roger laughed too. But he quickly sobered. "At least you love Hooke Manor and your father's other estates. You're interested in horses and the land and the people who live on it. And you have Adam to depend upon to help you run it after you become the Earl of Hooke. While I, on the other hand, am expected to give up my wasteful interests, such as painting and drawing, and take a hand in managing Bernhardt & Son."

Sebastian heard the dread in his friend's voice. Peter Bernhardt, Roger's father, had taken over the drapery store founded by his own father. Under his leadership, as the business had succeeded and grown, so had Peter's ambitions. Over a decade before, he had acquired a building on Oxford Street in London, and Bernhardt & Son, as it had been christened, had become one of several department stores located on the fashionable shopping street. It didn't matter to Peter Bernhardt that his son had little business acumen and no interest in being shut up in an office or a London store for hours, days, and weeks on end. Roger was Peter's son and, therefore, would assume his intended role in the business.

Roger turned and leaned his back against the fence. "I've talked to the ranch foreman. His name is Jake Foster. Jake knows of a man in Bozeman who escorts groups into the park. They sleep on cots in tents and travel from site to site. The tours last about ten days to two weeks. I believe I'll join one of them. The tours don't begin until after the snow melts which should be by late June." He looked toward the setting sun. "Perhaps sooner if the weather stays this warm."

"You're going by yourself?"

"Wouldn't have to. You could come. You and Amanda both. I'd be jolly well pleased to have you along. With any luck I could get some sketching done or perhaps I will just take it all in as a tourist and plan a return on my own when I can paint for as long as I'd like. There's a new hotel inside the park on the lake. I'm told it is rather fine. Maybe I'll choose to spend the rest of the summer there. The snows can come early in the autumn, so if I'm going to get the experience I came for, it'll have to be soon."

"You aren't tied to the ranch, Roger. You're my guest, but you are free to go and do whatever you like." He mimicked his friend, turning and leaning his back against the fence. "I envy you."

"*You* envy *me?*" Genuine surprise widened the other man's eyes.

"Yes. The way you see the world. You see things I miss entirely, I'll be bound. You observe the way the wind bends a tree or the particular green of the grass in a field. And that portrait you painted of my father? It captured him utterly in ways I can't even define." He shook his head. "What you can accomplish with the stroke of your brush . . ." He let the words fade into silence.

Roger placed a hand on Sebastian's shoulder. "My friend, you are good for my ego."

Smiling, the two men strolled away from the paddock in the direction of the house.

JOCELYN LEFT her brother's bedroom, a bundle of bandages and a washbasin in her hands. She had seen much improvement in William's wound over the past week. Perhaps she could spend less time worrying about him, and more enjoying her time at the ranch.

The front door opened as Jocelyn descended the stairs, and Sebastian Whitcombe and Roger Bernhardt appeared in the foyer.

"Ah, Miss Overstreet." Sebastian took a step toward her and stopped. "And how is your brother faring today?"

"Better." She stopped on the bottom step. "Dr. Grant has given him permission to leave his bed at last, as long as he is careful and does not overdo. Nothing strenuous, and he must use his crutches whenever he is up."

"Jolly good news, that," Roger said, grinning.

Over the past week, the two men had spent a few hours with her brother, broken into brief periods of time, but she had made herself absent during those visits. She didn't know what they'd spoken about. However, she'd noticed William's mood improved each time Sebastian came to see him, whether alone or with Roger. She was thankful for that.

"We will do our best to help make certain he does nothing he shouldn't. Won't we, Roger?"

She longed to tell Sebastian he should not concern himself, to say she could take care of her brother all on her own. But truth be told, she would need his help. His and Roger's and probably Amanda's as well. William's restlessness had been evident this evening as she'd changed the bandage on his leg. It wouldn't be long before he wouldn't need her at the ranch at all. He would be back to work, and she would be free to return to New York. Only she wasn't ready to leave the ranch. Not yet. She felt no concern for the management of Overstreet Shipping in her absence. She trusted her board of directors to see that the company ran smoothly. And if there was an emergency, she could be reached by telegram.

"Miss Joss!" Mrs. Adler's voice cut through the lengthening silence and jerked Jocelyn from her ruminations. "Wherever have you been?" The housekeeper strode forward, stretching out her arms to relieve Jocelyn of the basin and bandages. "You need to go rest yourself and let me do my job."

Jocelyn was tempted to remind Mrs. Adler that she was no longer twelve and needing told what to do. But there was great affection mingled with the housekeeper's desire to be in charge, so she couldn't be upset by it.

"Miss Overstreet, we were about to have a cup of tea with Amanda." Sebastian motioned toward the parlor. "Please join us."

A refusal rose in Jocelyn's throat even as she found herself nodding assent.

"Wonderful." He offered his arm, as if he were about to lead her to the dance floor at a ball.

Surprising herself yet again, she responded by placing her fingertips on the back of his wrist, and he walked her into the parlor. Dying rays of light coming through the windows were aided by lamps on several tables, giving the large room a warm, intimate glow.

"Miss Overstreet," Amanda said upon seeing them, "how good of you to join us."

"And with William's improved health, we hope to see more of you." Roger crossed to the sofa and sat near Amanda.

Sebastian guided Jocelyn to the sofa, then stepped back with a slight bow before walking to an empty chair.

Amanda poured tea into the waiting cups. "I overheard you tell Sebastian your brother is much improved and is allowed to leave his bedchamber at last. I shall be ever so happy when I get to meet him. I must say I am terribly curious about our host. I have many questions to ask Mr. Overstreet."

As Jocelyn took the proffered cup of tea from Amanda's hand, it occurred to her how very lovely, how close to utter perfection, the young Englishwoman was. Everything about Amanda Whitcombe was feminine, delicate, and refined. She doubted anyone would have used those adjectives to describe *her*. She was a woman, to be sure, but she wasn't delicate or refined. Oh, she had proper manners and mostly used them. She could attend a dance and not shame herself. She knew how to pour tea if required. But she was more accustomed to a boardroom than a ballroom. She spent more time in the company of men than with other women. She knew how to negotiate a business deal more than she knew how to make small conversation.

"Amanda," Roger said, drawing Jocelyn's attention in his direction, "I've decided to take a tour into the park at the end of next month, assuming the snow is gone by then. I'm told it should be. And I'd like you and Sebastian to come along." His gaze shifted to Jocelyn. "Perhaps Miss Overstreet would like to join us as well."

Jocelyn felt a flutter of excitement. She hadn't spent time in Yellowstone since she was a girl of fourteen, about eight years after the park had first opened. She remembered her father grumbling about the poachers, squatters, and vandals, and how ineffectual the superintendent was for letting the park be ill-treated by so many. Would she see many changes after fifteen years?

"What is it William said?" Sebastian set his cup and saucer on the low table before him. "Ah. I remember. He said we'll be roughing it when we go to the park."

"Roughing it." Amanda clapped her hands once. "Like the title of the Mark Twain book."

Sebastian leaned toward Jocelyn. "As you can see, Miss Overstreet, my sister has completely lost her heart to the American West. It has consumed her thoughts and much of her reading for the past eight years."

"Why so?" She looked toward the younger woman.

"Buffalo Bill brought his Wild West to England during the spring of Queen Victoria's Golden Jubilee. I'll never forget what we saw." Amanda's face shone with excitement. "Father said there were close to two hundred performers and nearly thirty thousand of us watching in the outdoor arena. There were cowboys and

Indians and Mexican vaqueros all on horses. At the opening of the show, they galloped around the arena, shouting and whooping. Later, the cowboys roped steers and rode bucking horses."

"Broncos," Sebastian inserted.

Amanda continued as if he hadn't spoken. "Wild Indians attacked the Deadwood stagecoach, and then Cody and his men came to the rescue. Annie Oakley shot a cigar out of the mouth of her husband."

Roger laughed. "A talent I would certainly discourage in a wife."

"It was all quite brilliant." Amanda gave a small toss of her head. "Even the queen agreed."

Beyond the windows, darkness had blanketed the barnyard. Jocelyn leaned to the side and adjusted the flame in the oil lamp. "You make me very sorry I didn't go to Chicago two years ago for the World's Columbian Exposition. I read that over three million people attended Buffalo Bill's show while it was there."

Amanda turned to her brother. "Perhaps we could go see him again while we're in America. He must be performing somewhere."

"If it's all right with you, dear sister, I should rather spend my time seeing the part of the country Colonel Cody helped make famous instead of visiting a big city and pretending we are in the Wild West."

Amanda released a sigh. "I suppose you are right." She covered her mouth as she yawned. "I'm frightfully tired all of a sudden. I'm afraid I shall have to retire early tonight."

Jocelyn set aside her cup and rose. "And I shall do

the same. On the ranch, we are ruled by the rising and setting of the sun." She offered a smile to the two men as they got to their feet. "I bid you all goodnight."

"Goodnight, Miss Overstreet," they said in unison.

But it was Sebastian Whitcombe's voice that seemed to reverberate in her chest as she made her way up the stairs.

Chapter Five

Sebastian discovered over the next five days that it wasn't an easy task to keep his promise to Jocelyn. Stopping her brother from overdoing was next to impossible once William was released from his bed. He mastered the use of the crutches in no time and moved around the house almost as quickly as anyone with two good legs under them. He wanted to be active again, wanted to be in the saddle and rounding up strays that had wandered into the nearby foothills and mountains.

And Sebastian longed to do the same.

Feeling sluggish after a Sunday dinner of roast beef with gravy, roasted potatoes, green beans, cornbread, and cups of strong coffee, Sebastian settled onto a chair in the shade provided by tall trees on the north side of the house. He was soon joined by William, and not long after, five cowboys made their way from the bunkhouse to the same spot, one of them carrying a guitar. Most of those same men had ridden into the town of Gibeon that morning to attend church, while Sebastian, his sister, and Roger had remained at the ranch, holding a quieter, private service with Jocelyn and William.

"Chuck did himself proud today," Jake Foster, the foreman, said as he leaned against a tree trunk.

"Shore nuf," the young cowboy with the guitar answered, strumming a few notes.

"Go on, Logan," Jake said. "Play us somethin'."

Logan Coe nodded, strummed the guitar a couple of times, then began. "'Oh, give me a home where the buffalo roam, where the deer and antelope play.'"

Other voices joined in. "'Where never is heard a discouraging word and the sky is not clouded all day.'"

It was for a moment like this Sebastian had crossed an ocean. He grinned, surprised by how good the men sounded, their voices blending together. Listening, he could imagine them seated around a campfire at night, cattle grazing amid the sagebrush, the night sky twinkling with stars.

If what he'd read was true, the life these men led was dying. Perhaps not in a decade. Perhaps not in two decades. Perhaps not even in three. But many who wrote about the American West seemed sure it couldn't last. The buffalo were almost extinct. The coming of the railroad had ended the need for the long cattle drives of yore. Cities thrived along the Pacific coast.

It seemed to Sebastian that hardly anything changed in England. Titles got passed from fathers to eldest sons. Young women came out in society and immediately searched for a husband of rank or fortune, preferably both. Good society was made up of the same families, and so wherever a man went, he was in the same crowd

—with the possible exception of the American heiresses who had married into the aristocracy. In recent years, those marriages had shaken things up, at least a little.

Thankfully, his father hadn't insisted Sebastian marry for money. A dowery was a good thing, of course, but Hooke Manor wasn't in dire need of an influx of cash. No, what the earl wanted was for his heir to sire the next heir. And soon. He wanted to guarantee his title and estate would remain in the Whitcombe family for generations to come.

Meaning, nothing would change.

Movement off to the right caught Sebastian's attention, pulling him from thoughts of England. As his eyes refocused, he realized it was Jocelyn Overstreet, leaving the barn, leading a saddle horse behind her. She had changed from the pale yellow dress she'd worn that morning for their home church service. Now she wore a tan blouse with a dark brown skirt. In fact, if he wasn't mistaken, it was a split skirt, similar to the ones occasionally seen in London on women riding bicycles.

As if to confirm his suspicion, Jocelyn gathered the reins, put her left foot in the stirrup, and stepped up, throwing her right leg over the saddle.

"By Jove," he whispered beneath his breath.

William nudged him in the arm. "You should go with her. You've been talking about exploring on horseback."

"But I—"

"Jocelyn!" William called to his sister before she could nudge her mount into action.

She turned the horse toward them.

"Wait up! Sebastian would like to ride with you."

Sebastian thought to object but realized he didn't want to object. He was eager to ride along with Jocelyn.

Still looking at his sister, William called, "I'll have one of the boys saddle a mount while he changes out of his Sunday duds." He grinned as he gave Sebastian's arm another shove. "Get going. Tom, get a horse ready for Sebastian, will you? One with some speed on him."

"Yes, sir." The cowboy hopped up and hurried toward the barn.

There wasn't anything Sebastian could do except rise and go to his room to change clothes.

Trapped.

While walking to the barn, Jocelyn had entertained the belief she could get away by herself for a short while. To simply enjoy a gallop across the land. To quit worrying about her brother and the ranch. Out of politeness, she'd invited Amanda Whitcombe to join her and had been relieved when the younger woman declined. But now she would be riding with Amanda's brother instead.

Trapped, indeed.

Then again, none of the three British guests were as intolerable as Jocelyn had expected them to be on the day they'd all arrived at the ranch. Amanda was sweet and vivacious, if a bit too talkative at times. Roger was a man of few words who slipped away whenever the "light was right" to sketch or to paint. And Sebastian? He'd been more than a little helpful with William. As William improved, the viscount and her brother had spent numerous hours talking about their school years and laughing about some of their pranks. She was forced to admit Sebastian wasn't stuffy or pompous as she'd expected him to be. Reserved at times, perhaps. But never pompous.

About the same time Tom Flores exited the barn leading a tall palomino gelding, Sebastian Whitcombe came out the front door of the house. He had changed into a blue shirt, denim trousers, and boots. Obviously all new. He also wore a wide-brimmed Stetson over his dark hair. The hat was new as well. The two men met near where Jocelyn waited astride her favorite mare, Bella.

"This here's Goldrush." Tom held out the gelding's reins to Sebastian.

"Goldrush," Sebastian repeated. "I like that." He ran a hand along the horse's neck and appreciation lit his expression.

Jocelyn wasn't surprised he had a keen eye for horse-flesh. William had told her about the Earl of Hooke's stables, including the family's hopes for a Grand National contender in their near future.

Sebastian glanced at her. "I've seen your western saddles in photographs and paintings, but I've never sat in one." Gathering the reins, he mounted Goldrush. "Wider seat." He shifted. "Heavier too, I'll be bound."

"You'll find it more comfortable for long rides. The seat distributes the rider's weight over a greater area than the type of saddles you use in England or that riders use back east." She arched an eyebrow. "And if you ever have cause to rope a cow, that saddle will help both you and the horse control it."

"I rather like the sound of that, roping a cow."

She swallowed the laugh rising in her throat. "Once Billy's back on his feet, I'm sure he'll be glad to teach you." *Try* to teach him is what she wanted to say. She couldn't imagine a British viscount roping cattle under a hot sun. Sebastian might say he wanted the western ranch experience, but she expected him to change his mind once it became too real, too hard, too dusty, too sweaty.

Although he does look nice in his new duds. Especially that Stetson.

"Shall we be off?" Sebastian asked.

Realizing she'd studied his appearance far too long, Jocelyn nudged the mare into a walk. Moments later, Sebastian caught up with her, but he didn't say anything. She was grateful for his silence. At least at first. But after a while, it was Jocelyn herself who felt the need to speak.

"Do you ride often in England?"

"I do. With my brother Adam. He manages the estate and the stables. He's the expert with horses."

"Your brother? I thought I understood from Billy that Amanda is your only sibling."

He stared toward the mountains. "Adam is my half-brother." He paused, then added, "He was born before my mother and father married. To another woman."

It took a few moments for her to understand his meaning. When she did, she felt the heat rise in her cheeks. "And you say he manages your father's estate?"

"Yes. We grew up together. And in every way that matters, Adam is my true brother. Mine and Amanda's." He glanced her way. As if to challenge her to say otherwise.

She suspected he had done a great deal of that through the years, challenging those who would disrespect his illegitimate half-brother. Perhaps there had been those in Sebastian's class who'd thought less of him because of Adam. It was much the same in New York's high society, but not so here in the West. People were judged for their character, for their behavior, more than anything else.

"Your brother is lucky to have you," she replied at last before pressing her heels against Bella's ribs.

The mare broke into a trot, then a slow canter, and eventually into a gallop. Jocelyn leaned forward. The wind caught her hat and blew it off her head. It bounced against her back, held in place by the tie around her neck. Laughter burbled up inside of her and escaped through smiling lips.

How long had it been since she'd ridden with such abandon? Years. Not since her last visit to Eden's Gate. She rode occasionally in Central Park, but it wasn't the same, especially since she was expected to ride sidesaddle in that setting. She *detested* the sidesaddle. And the whole point of riding in Central Park was to be seen by others. Here on Eden's Gate, the point was to feel exhilarated.

As they neared the base of the tree-covered mountain, Jocelyn reined in, drawing Bella down to a walk.

When she glanced to her left, she found Sebastian grinning at her. He looked the same way she felt.

"I must say, Miss Overstreet. You surprise me."

"Surprise you?" She pushed loose strands of hair back from her face. "Why?"

"I'm not sure. But William never described this woman I see before me when he talked about you while we were at school or in his letters after."

Something strange coiled in Jocelyn's stomach. "Billy talked about me?"

"We *all* talked about our siblings. Sisters especially. Particularly the younger ones like you and Amanda."

"I daresay you weren't always very nice to your sisters."

He laughed softly. "I daresay you're right. We were boys about to become men without as many brains as we thought we had. We weren't always nice, and we definitely said too much about the sisters we had—and have—a duty to love and protect."

"'Even a fool,'" she quoted, "'when he holdeth his peace, is counted wise: And he that shutteth his lips is esteemed a man of understanding.'"

Sebastian looked surprised an instant before robust laughter burst from his lips.

Heat rose in Jocelyn's cheeks a second time, and she wished she'd followed the proverb's advice herself. Silence would have been more prudent, even if he didn't seem insulted.

"Let's continue, Miss Overstreet. I want to see more of Eden's Gate, and I suspect you are as good a guide as William will be once he's allowed to ride again."

Chapter Six

The next morning, feeling a trifle saddle sore from the previous day's ride, Jocelyn opened the door to the dark-paneled study that had once been her father's domain. Now the room served as William's office, the place where he conducted business and oversaw the running of Eden's Gate. Her brother was seated at the desk, a ledger open before him.

"Mrs. Adler said you would be in here." She entered the room and sat opposite him.

"Amazing how things can pile up when a man's indisposed. It's not even a month since that buffalo got his horn in me, and it'll take me forever to make sense of what's been done and not done while I was down."

Jocelyn suspected the issues of what had been done and not done went back further than a month. "Isn't it time you tell me what's been going on with the ranch?"

"You know what's been going on. I got gored. It could've been worse, but I survived and I kept my leg. Now I'm getting better."

Jocelyn sighed. "That isn't what I mean, and you know it. You're in some kind of financial trouble. That's why you rented out the house to Sebastian Whitcombe."

"That's *one* reason I rented the house." William closed the ledger. "We've had a rough few years. A couple of hard winters added to the financial panic of 'ninety-three and the economic depression that's still around because of it. We aren't getting the same price for beef on the hoof we were getting before."

Jocelyn nodded. She should have realized the financial panic hadn't affected only those in the east. The economic crisis had been of great concern to Overstreet Shipping, although wise decisions by Jocelyn and her board of directors had minimized the financial hardships. "Why didn't you tell me? You could have written. We have the resources."

"*You* have the resources. But you've also got your hands full. The ranch is my concern. We settled that years ago."

"You're in charge of the ranch, but that doesn't mean it isn't of concern to me. I love Eden's Gate." She leaned forward. "And I love you."

Her brother dipped his head forward and massaged his forehead with his fingertips. When he looked up, his expression was vulnerable. "But you haven't come for a visit in six years."

"I know." Regret warmed her chest. "I always meant to, but . . ."

"But there was always something more important to do first."

"I'm here now, Billy."

"Yes, you're here now."

"Will you allow me to help?"

He shrugged.

"Numbers make sense to me." She motioned to the ledger. "I have a good head for business."

"Father always said that about you." He smiled at her. "It's a pretty head, sis. It shouldn't be shut up in a stuffy old boardroom all the time. If you're going to live in New York City, you should at least enjoy yourself sometimes. Go to balls and wear fancy dresses."

She waved away his comment. "The Overstreets have money, Billy, but we aren't the Vanderbilts. And we have no real position in society."

"Real enough that you should be married by now."

Jocelyn stiffened. "Are you calling me an old maid?"

"I wouldn't dare."

She felt the tension leave her shoulders as quickly as it had come. However, while her brother might not call her a spinster, at twenty-nine, she could hardly think of herself otherwise. Once, not long after their father died, she'd received a proposal of marriage. She'd tried to think she was in love with Robert Burnett, the son of an Overstreet Shipping board member. But in the end, she'd known she didn't love Robert any more than he loved her. He'd wanted an acquisition, not a marriage.

"Are you happy, Jocelyn?"

Pulled from her thoughts, she tilted her chin. "I am as happy as I have any right to be."

"How happy is that?"

She didn't know how to answer him and so made do with a slow shake of her head.

"Don't rush back to New York just because I'm getting better. Stay for the summer."

"I told my assistant I would return in six to eight weeks, unless your recovery took longer."

"My recovery will definitely take longer. I'm sure of it. It'll be at least September before I can get by without you. Tell Paul Danvers not to expect you until the fall. The board of directors can manage well enough without you until then."

Love for William welled in her heart, and tears stung her eyes. "I have missed you, Billy. And I've missed the ranch. I didn't know how much until my hired coach rolled into the valley." She brushed away the tears clinging to her eyelashes. "It would be nice to spend the summer with you."

He pushed the ledger toward her. "You could help me get the accounts in order, like you said. I'm not asking for your money, but maybe you could help me get a better handle on expenses and such."

"It isn't just *my* money, Billy. Overstreet Shipping belongs to us both. And I would like to help."

"Then stay. The ranch is ours as well. Put the accounts in order. That'll make you happy. All those numbers in nice, neat columns. Then take long rides. That'll make you even happier. You might even help with the branding. You loved that as a girl. And participate in the roundup when it's time to ship the cows and calves off to market."

Jocelyn laughed softly. "It was always hard for me to say no to you, big brother."

"That's as it should be, little sister."

"All right. I'll let the board know I'll stay in Idaho until the fall."

———————

SEBASTIAN STOOD ON THE PORCH, staring into the distance. But his thoughts had returned once more to the ride he'd taken with Jocelyn the previous day. William's sister was an intriguing woman. She had an air of confidence about her that was lacking in most others of her sex. Of course, she was more mature than the majority of marriageable young women back in England. A good ten years older than most.

He wondered why she'd never married. She was certainly attractive enough to have had plenty of suitors. Quite above the average in appearance, to be sure. While her figure was undeniably exquisite, it was her eyes that drew his attention. The gold flecks in the hazel depths seemed to sparkle with intelligence. He supposed that intelligence—added to her confident demeanor—might put some men off. But not him.

"Sebastian?"

At the sound of Amanda's voice, he turned toward the front door.

"Am I disturbing you?"

"Not at all."

She held up a letter and envelope. "I've just heard from a friend of mine. Her letter went first to England. Father forwarded it here. It's really quite extraordinary."

"What is?"

"My friend, Olivia Mason. Do you remember her?"

She paused only a second before continuing, "She married an American five years ago. Against her mother's strenuous objections, I might add. Anyway, her last name is Crawford now. Like us, she attended Buffalo Bill's Wild West exhibition during the Queen's Jubilee. I saw her there. What I didn't know is that was where she met the man she married. He was one of the performers. It turns out he raised the Palouse horses that performed in the show. She remembered how much I admired the spotted horses when I saw them and sent me a photograph of one of their mares and two foals." She pulled the photograph from the envelope and held it toward him. "Olivia writes that only some of the Nez Perce's horses survived after the war in 1877, and her husband's family was fortunate enough to acquire part of the herd that escaped in a place called Wallowa Valley."

Sebastian looked at the photograph, suppressing the urge to ask his sister to get to the point. He hoped there was one.

As if in answer, Amanda said, "I should like to go visit Olivia and her husband in the state of Washington."

"You what?"

"It isn't that far, according to Mr. Kincaid. He said I would have to take a coach north into Montana. From there I can take a train across the top of Idaho and into Washington."

"You sound as if you know where those places are. And even if you do, I do not. Nor do I know Olivia Mason or Crawford or whatever her name is. I most certainly do not know her husband. I cannot allow you to go traipsing off alone around the American West. It's not called the *Wild* West for nothing."

Amanda's eyes narrowed, a warning that she was prepared to fight to get her way. "I have no intention of *traipsing* anywhere, alone or otherwise. I will contact Olivia to let her know I am in Idaho at this very moment. I will ascertain if a visit is in order and make certain I am welcome on her husband's ranch. Only then would I make plans to go visit her."

"But—"

"*And* I have already asked Roger if he would escort me to Washington. Since he cannot go into the park until the very end of June or early July, he said he would be happy to accompany me."

"You asked Roger without speaking to me first?"

She laughed. "Gracious. You sound as if you mean to forbid me to go."

"Don't tempt me," he replied gruffly.

"Oh, dear brother. Don't be stuffy. And for pity's sake, don't behave like Father. We came to America to experience the Wild West before it is completely gone. You know how taken I was with the Palouse horses in London. I never imagined a friend of mine might offer me the opportunity to see them up close while I am here. You wouldn't refuse me such an experience."

"You're sure Roger doesn't mind?"

"I am sure. He told me so himself, and you know Roger. He wouldn't say yes if he didn't mean it."

"It seems you've thought of everything, but I still want to talk with him before I agree to it."

"Sebastian." She drew out his name. "I am not a child."

"And because you are not a child, you will allow me to talk to him without an argument." He leaned forward and kissed her forehead. "Please."

"You are exasperating."

"I try my best."

She smiled again. "You succeed."

Chapter Seven

Eight days later, on the day of Amanda and Roger's departure for Washington, Jocelyn stood in the yard, a hand shielding her eyes from the bright morning sunlight.

"Do take care of my brother while I'm away," Amanda said.

Jocelyn's gaze slipped to Sebastian. The man was hardly in need of a caretaker.

"We shan't be gone long," Amanda added. "Three weeks at most."

Looking toward Sebastian, Roger said, "We'll be back before it's time for all of us to head into the park."

Sebastian nodded.

"Better get going, folks," the driver said from his high seat. "We got us a lot of miles to cover."

Amanda and Roger promptly climbed into the coach, and within minutes, they were away, dust rising behind the vehicle as the horses picked up the pace.

"Our father would not approve," Sebastian said softly.

"Of what?" Jocelyn asked.

He faced her. "I should have gone with her."

"Why?"

He gave his head a slight shake.

She resisted the urge to touch his arm. "I was a year younger than Amanda when I took the reins of Overstreet Shipping. I haven't known you or your sister long, but I'm quite certain she is able to manage well enough on her own. And she isn't alone. Mr. Bernhardt is with her."

"My sister is a dreamer. Always with her head in the clouds. I suspect you are more levelheaded."

Perhaps his words were meant as a compliment, but they irritated instead. Or perhaps they wounded. Jocelyn wasn't *all* business. She had her own dreams and wishes. Or she had once.

"If you'll excuse me, Miss Overstreet. I promised Logan I would assist him with something in the barn."

"Of course." She watched as Sebastian strode away, then she turned and walked to the porch where William sat, his feet propped on a second chair to keep his right leg raised, per the doctor's orders. Without a word, she sat in another nearby chair.

"Sebastian's always been protective of Amanda," he said. "You should have heard him talk about her when we were in school."

"Did you talk about me to him?" She knew the answer. Sebastian had admitted as much to her on their ride the previous week.

"Sure, but it was different. You were on the other side of the ocean, and we went months without seeing each other. Sebastian and Amanda were together most of the time when he was away from school so he had plenty of stories to tell me and the other lads. Another way it was different is because there's only three years between you and me. There's ten years between them. Sebastian still thinks of Amanda as a young girl, even now. He doesn't always recognize she's become a woman."

"How could he not recognize it?"

William shrugged. "Always the little sister, perhaps."

A gust of wind—fresh and cool—caused the trees at the side of the house to bob and dance for a few moments. The mellow lowing of cattle drifted to them from a distance. A horse in the nearby corral huffed and stomped a hoof. Familiar sounds. Soothing sounds.

Jocelyn released a sigh and closed her eyes. "I love mornings on Eden's Gate."

"Yeah. It's not like this in New York. Right? London either. Too much going on in the cities. Too much noise. Too many people."

She opened her eyes to see Sebastian ride Goldrush out of the barn and turn the horse east toward the mountain range. "There was a time I found the bustle of the city invigorating," she said.

"But no more? You don't miss being there?"

"I . . . I'm not sure."

"You could sell the company. You could sell it and move back to Idaho."

"Sell Overstreet Shipping?" She looked at her

brother. "Papa would roll over in his grave to hear you say that."

"He would care more about your happiness. Dad loved the company, sure, but he didn't expect us to be like him."

Longing stung Jocelyn's chest. Missing Eden's Gate. Missing her parents.

How would her life be different if her mother were still alive? Jocelyn had been fourteen when she passed, only a few months after the family's visit to Yellowstone. Jocelyn had thought she was grown up at the time, but looking back, she'd still been a child. She'd stayed close to her father after her mother's death. Was that the real reason she'd spent so much time at Overstreet Shipping as a girl and young woman? Not because she loved learning to run the business but because she'd loved being with Papa and was afraid she might lose him too.

"You're here for the summer," William said. "That's already decided. Now put Overstreet Shipping out of your head for the next few months. See what it's like to live without it. Breathe the fresh air. Spend time with a good book." He jerked his head toward the mountains. "Take another ride with Sebastian."

She couldn't help smiling. "What makes you like him so much?"

"Despite being a nob, he's a good fellow. He was never unkind to the American nobody who dared attend Eton."

His answer surprised her. She'd never heard him speak like that about his years in England. "Was it so bad, Billy? Eton?"

He stared into the distance. As if looking back in time. "Not all bad. Not all the time. But it was bad enough."

"I never understood why Papa made that choice for you."

"I don't know either. I never figured it out, and he never said. It wasn't a punishment, although it felt that way when I was thirteen." He forced a chuckle. "Didn't help that I got seasick at the first sight of a wave."

She laughed with him to lighten the mood. Still, she suspected there was much William hadn't told her about his boyhood years in England.

SEBASTIAN DISMOUNTED on a hillside and stared across the green valley. He could just make out the Overstreet house and outbuildings in the distance. He couldn't say how many miles he'd ridden. He'd been lost in his own thoughts. To the south of him, he saw a small herd of cattle—Herefords—being moved by about five or six Eden's Gate cowboys.

Odd, that. British cattle here on this American ranch. He'd expected to find Texas longhorns, but William said Eden's Gate had begun replacing the longhorns with Herefords about fifteen years before. There were no longhorns left on the ranch. Like the buffalo, they were disappearing from the landscape.

There was something to be said for how little things changed in England, he supposed. At least in his circles. Then again, he'd felt restless there and had wanted this experience in the American West. However, when it came down to it, his roots were at Hooke Manor. His life was in England. In England . . . with a wife.

He released a deep sigh. Marriage was an acceptable notion—in theory.

Once again, the image of William's sister drifted into his thoughts. But when he imagined introducing her to his father as the future Countess of Hooke, he almost laughed. The earl would be apoplectic. An American? That would be bad enough in his father's mind. But a woman who managed a shipping company? A woman in trade? The earl might have a stroke over the possibility.

As he remounted the gelding, Sebastian thought of his half-brother Adam and Adam's wife, Eliza. The couple had met by chance in the stables on her father's estate. She was a lady with prospects and he the natural son of an earl with little to offer. But they'd fallen in love against all reason and against the violent objections of her father. But they were now happily married. Ridiculously so, from what Sebastian had observed. In fact, if he were honest, he would admit to feeling some envy over Adam's domestic bliss.

He turned Goldrush down the hillside, heading in the direction of the cowboys and the herd of cattle. He might as well ride along with them. That's why he was here. To live like one of the boys on this ranch.

When the horse reached level ground, Sebastian nudged him into a canter, then a gallop. Goldrush's legs ate up the ground, reminding Sebastian once again of his half-brother and the long rides they'd taken, racing each other across the fields of Hooke Manor. Adam had often won but not always. These days he was riding beside his bride, and Sebastian would wager he let Eliza win, more often than not.

As Sebastian drew closer to the cattle, he slowed Goldrush to a walk. Logan Coe raised an arm to wave him forward. When Sebastian reached him, the cowboy said, "I was wonderin' when you were gonna get tired of hangin' around the homestead. All that idleness makes a man itch." Logan wiggled his shoulders and scrunched his face, as if he needed to scratch somewhere.

Sebastian nodded but said nothing.

"Well, fall in at the back of the herd. Greenhorns get to eat dust." Logan grinned as he tugged at the brim of his hat.

"I suppose that is fair." Sebastian turned his gelding toward the far end of the small herd.

The other cowboys greeted him as he moved into position. He knew all their faces, but he hadn't managed to learn all their names yet. That was going to change. With Amanda off on her own adventure, accompanied by Roger, Sebastian was free to spend his days any way he chose. He chose to spend it with these men.

He slowed his horse, falling in beside the foreman. "Where are you taking them, Jake?"

"We're moving them to the west range. There's signs of a grizzly back where they were." He jerked his head, indicating the direction they'd come from. "Would just as soon the bear doesn't get a taste for beef on the hoof."

Sebastian wondered if they had a lot of trouble with

bears and buffalo, but he would have to ask later. For now he made himself useful, turning Goldrush after a couple of cows falling behind the rest of the herd.

Logan was right about one thing. He would be eating plenty of dust.

Chapter Eight

The morning after Amanda's and Roger's departure, Jocelyn sat at the writing desk in her second-floor bedroom, sunrise spilling through the eastern window, brightening the white of her nightgown where the hem puddled on the floor.

June 12, 1895

   Dear Paul,

   I write to inform you of my intention to remain in Idaho until fall. While William is expected to make a full recovery, I believe it is better for me to stay with him throughout the summer for a number of reasons.

   Please advise the board of directors I have complete faith in their ability to handle anything of urgent nature that should arise at Overstreet Shipping. I do not expect that will happen. I have even more faith in you to make certain no drastic changes are made without my approval. If necessary, you will be able to reach me through the telegraph office in Gibeon which is only an hour away.

I trust you to keep me informed of anything needing my personal attention. I may be away from the ranch for a two week period in July but should otherwise be reachable in a reasonable amount of time.

Thank you for all you do at Overstreet Shipping. You have proven yourself a valuable asset to the company and to me personally.

With regards,

Jocelyn Overstreet

It had taken her better than a week to write this letter after telling William she would. Had she expected to change her mind? Perhaps. But it was done now. She hadn't changed her mind. Her intention to remain in Idaho would be made clear to the board of directors, and she felt a little lighter because of it.

Brushing a hank of hair off her shoulder, she rose and walked to the window, squinting against the bright morning light. To her surprise, she saw William, on his crutches, with Sebastian, walking toward the barn. Surely her brother wasn't intending to ride. No, it was more likely he was simply talking to his friend before Sebastian headed out for another day with the Eden's Gate ranch hands. Another day with Sebastian gone from the ranch house from dawn to dusk.

Why did that feel all wrong?

She whirled from the window and made short shrift of her morning ablutions. In no time at all, she was dressed in a loose-fitted blouse, riding skirt, and boots. Her hair was quickly captured in a single braid down her back and covered with her floppy-brimmed hat.

Then she was out the door. She found the two men inside the barn, Sebastian brushing Goldrush while William observed from nearby. She called a greeting as she strode toward them.

William glanced her way. "You're up early."

"I've been up a long while. I had a letter to write." She glanced in Sebastian's direction. "What are the boys doing today?"

William answered, "Moving more cattle to the west grazing land."

"More signs of the grizzly?"

"Yes, and nearer than we like to see." He jerked his head toward the stall that held Bella. "If you plan to join the boys, take your rifle. I don't want you out there without it."

Sebastian asked, "Have you a rifle for me?"

"Sure. But can you shoot without killing an innocent bystander?"

"Who shot the most birds on our hunts in England?" Sebastian challenged. "Not to mention the stags I brought down at the manor."

William laughed. "You're right. I forgot." He looked at Jocelyn. "Sebastian's got a keen eye. I was joking when I asked if he could shoot."

She acknowledged the words with a nod.

Her brother turned back to his friend. "Been a long time since we went hunting together."

"Too long."

"We'll have to change that while you're here."

"Agreed." Sebastian placed a hand on William's shoulder.

Jocelyn's heart warmed as she remembered her brother's words about Sebastian's kindness to him all those years ago. She hadn't known about their friendship back then, but she was thankful for it now.

"I'd better get my horse," she said softly before walking to Bella's stall.

By the time she had the mare brushed, bridled, and saddled, Sebastian had done the same with Goldrush. Outside the barn, sounds told her the cowboys were also readying their mounts and preparing for the day ahead.

William shouted, "Tom, you out there?

"Yes, sir." Tom Flores stepped into view.

"Get rifles for both Sebastian and Jocelyn. They're going to accompany you men today."

Tom tugged on his hat brim. "Yes, sir."

Excitement and a touch of trepidation stirred in Jocelyn's chest. When her brother had urged her to remain at the ranch for the summer, he'd mentioned she could help with roundup and branding. But that had been before a grizzly was known to be roaming on Eden's Gate land. She'd seen one of the great bears years ago, from a distance, and the memory of it still made her shiver.

"Did you eat breakfast?" William asked, pulling her attention back to him.

"I had tea and toast before writing my letter."

"Not much to ride on."

"No time for more. I'll be fine."

Her brother shook his head. "Dad told me you were always in a hurry. Never wanted to be left behind. You would rather starve than miss out."

"I guess I was like that," she answered softly. When had that changed? In New York, in a business setting, she was thoughtful, methodical, reasonable. Her father had appreciated those qualities in her. They had served her well when managing a shipping concern. But here, on this ranch—

"You're still like that." William patted Bella's neck. "You be careful out here. You hear?"

She kissed her brother's cheek. "I hear." Then she stepped into the saddle and rode out of the barn.

SEBASTIAN GATHERED THE REINS, preparing to mount Goldrush.

"Sebastian, wait."

He turned toward his friend, catching the concern in his eyes.

"Keep an eye out for that grizzly." Gruffness laced William's words.

Sebastian understood what he really meant to say. Keep an eye out for Jocelyn. Protect her. See that she came to no harm. "I will." He stepped into the saddle.

They rode out, seven men and one woman, pairing into twos with Sebastian and Jocelyn bringing up the rear.

"Eating dust from the start," Sebastian said beneath his breath.

"What?" Jocelyn looked over at him.

He chuckled. "Nothing important."

"Oh." She laughed too. "You've received greenhorn treatment, haven't you? Back of the herd yesterday?"

"Yes, but to be honest, the men have been rather more welcoming than I expected. I am a foreigner and, indeed, a greenhorn when it comes to ranching." His smile broadened. "If I'm not mistaken, I do believe even Mrs. Adler has warmed to me a little."

The riders ahead of them quickened the pace, putting an end to the conversation, and soon they were all cantering across the countryside. Goldrush needed no direction from his rider. The gelding was content to follow the other horses, leaving Sebastian free to consider the woman riding next to him.

She was pretty at any time and by any standard, but there was something extraordinary about her face at this moment. He wished he could define it, understand it. She intrigued him, this woman, unlike any other he'd known. He'd met her for the first time a mere three weeks ago. Except for the day they'd ridden together when she'd shown him the extent of Eden's Gate Ranch, their interactions had been too brief to suit him. Most days they'd eaten supper together, in the company of his sister and Roger and, in this last week, William. But the conversations around the table each night had done little to satisfy his growing interest in her. She wasn't a chatterbox like Amanda. Not shy, exactly. Just measured with her words. He liked that about her.

Up ahead, Jake raised a hand, and the group slowed their horses to a walk. Sebastian stood in his stirrups and spied the red-brown cattle grazing not far ahead.

"Fan out, men," Jake called, "and let's start 'em moving."

Squinting into the morning sun, Jocelyn stared toward the far side of the herd. "Look, Mr. Whitcombe." She pointed to several cows headed for a copse of trees. "Let's get them."

His pulse quickened, and he wasn't sure if the cause was the thought of galloping across this land to bring back some rebellious cows or if it was simply her invitation to join him in the chase. "I'm with you." He kicked his horse into action.

Jocelyn led the way, her body forward over the pommel. Her hat blew off her head, and as he'd seen before, it bounced against her back, made wild by the wind. It reminded him of a painting by Frederic Remington, although the artist's work usually featured cavalrymen or cowboys or Indians. Not a woman like Jocelyn Overstreet.

By heaven! He loved this.

He leaned low and urged more speed from Goldrush. Little by little, they gained on Jocelyn and the mare. He saw her glance back at him and heard her laugh of delight. He was so intent on catching and passing her that he almost missed the way she brought her horse to an abrupt halt.

"Stop, Sebastian!"

He reacted more to the tone of her voice than to the actual words. Pulling on the reins, he brought Goldrush to a sliding halt, causing dust and dirt to fly up around them. Sebastian started to turn toward Jocelyn, but other sounds stopped him. The frightened complaint of cows and, then, a growl that caused the hair to stand on the back of his neck.

"Back your horse up," Jocelyn said in a low but steady voice. "Slowly."

As he obeyed, he saw the massive bear between two trees perhaps eighty yards ahead of them. Thankfully, the grizzly didn't seem ready to give chase to the escaping cattle. Or, for that matter, to him and Jocelyn.

He heard the sounds, almost like a chorus, of rifles being prepared to fire. That's when he realized more of the Eden's Gate cowboys had joined them on the ridge.

"Miss Joss," Logan Coe said softly. "It would make us a sight happier if you get yourself on back to the herd. You and Sebastian keep the cows movin'. I reckon that there bear has himself one of 'em to eat already, back among the trees. We don't want him gettin' any more. Rocky, you go with Miss Joss, too. The boss will want her kept safe above anything."

Sebastian knew lots about racing horses and a little about raising cattle. But bears? There hadn't been bears in England in seven hundred years, except possibly in the London Zoological Gardens. And he would wager there'd never been a bear like the one he saw before him.

As if in reply, the grizzly shook its head back and forth, raising one front paw off the ground, then the other. It huffed, then growled, louder this time. Even from this distance, Sebastian felt the threat of the beast.

"Miss Joss," Jake Foster said, "your brother will have my hide if you don't make yourself scarce."

Jocelyn slipped her rifle from the scabbard. "I'm not

going anywhere, Jake." There was determination in the set of her shoulders and the tilt of her jaw.

Sebastian was secretly glad for her decision. He didn't want to miss this. He wasn't ready to ride away from whatever would happen next. Matching Jocelyn and the cowboys, he withdrew his rifle and pointed it toward the great bear.

Did the grizzly perceive the threat? He seemed to. Snout pointed upward, he roared as he rose onto his hind legs. A chill went through Sebastian. Great heavens! How tall was it? Eight feet? Nine? And its paws. Even from this distance, he could tell how massive they were. He imagined that bear taking a swipe at a man. Who could survive such an encounter? He glanced toward Jocelyn, wondering if he'd been wrong not to escort her to safety. But the expression she wore now told him any such attempt would have been useless. His gaze followed hers back to the bear.

The grizzly dropped to all fours and charged forward with surprising speed. The ground thundered beneath it, like the earth shaking from a passing train. Goldrush reacted with a snort and a quick hop backward. Heart pounding and mouth dry, Sebastian steadied his horse even as he leveled the rifle. As he squeezed the trigger, other rifles fired around him.

It was strange, the way Sebastian felt at the moment the grizzly thudded to the ground, a cloud of dust rising up around it. Triumphant. Yet profoundly sad. Thankful there'd been enough distance between bear and riders to keep them safe. Surprise no horse had thrown its rider. Glad he'd been there for the kill. Sorry such a magnificent beast had to die. He looked over at Jocelyn once again.

"Is it really dead?" she asked softly.

"I believe so."

She met his gaze. "I . . . I was terrified when it charged us."

"Were you? You didn't look it."

A shaky smile bowed her lips. "I've never seen a grizzly up that close before."

"And it's a sight I shall never forget." Neither would he forget the sight of Jocelyn as she'd been moments before. Brave and full of resolve. Exceptional. Remarkable.

Jake intruded on his thoughts. "Logan, go help Rocky with the cattle. We're lucky they haven't run to kingdom come."

"What will you do with the bear?" Jocelyn asked.

"I'll send a wagon back later today. Don't want the vultures to get to it."

No, they didn't want the vultures to get to it. And Sebastian suspected there would be a new bearskin rug in one of the bedrooms of the ranch house after today.

Dear Adam,

I apologize for not writing to you for several weeks. After our safe arrival in New York City, which you know about if you've received my previous letter, we boarded a train bound for a town called Pocatello. From there we hired a private coach (I hired a horse so I could ride) to bring us to the Overstreet ranch. It's called Eden's Gate, and I understand perfectly the reason why. It does seem to border on heaven itself.

The space, brother. The absolute width and breadth of everything. One expects it, having looked at maps and calculated the distances on the same. And yet, one does not completely comprehend the size of this country until it is seen in person.

There are English estates with perhaps as many acres as make up Eden's Gate, although not many of them. Surely none of them hold as many cattle. The nearby mountain ranges are part of the Rocky Mountains. I read that the Rockies (as they are also called) stretch for three thousand miles, reaching from Canada in the north to the territory of New Mexico in the south. Three thousand miles of granite peaks and trees. Forbidding mountains that would have halted the connecting of one coast to another if not for brave pioneers who discovered ways through them.

Upon our arrival, we learned William Overstreet had suffered an injury. His leg was gored by an American bison. We have not seen a buffalo for ourselves. Perhaps we will see one when we go into the park next month. That is likely our best opportunity.

Today, I was out with the cowboys (Adam, you would enjoy these men a great deal), moving a small herd of cattle from one part of the ranch to another, when we encountered a grizzly bear. Never have I seen anything like it. Because it would have killed more cattle if left to roam the range, it had to be killed. I will never forget the moment it fell. Never.

William is much improved from when we first arrived. He is able to get around on crutches now and fully expects to be riding by the end of next week. I am surprised the doctor and his sister have managed to keep him off a horse this long.

His sister, Jocelyn Overstreet, is unlike any woman I have met before. She runs the family's shipping company, the one William was expected to take over from their father. She is bright, as you would expect of a woman in commerce. I suspect she can be great fun, given the right opportunities. I am uncertain if she would appreciate my assessment. She is independent in her thinking and actions. I keep wondering what Father would think of her. I cannot imagine he would approve. But is it not strange that I wonder about it? Often.

I have not mentioned how pretty she is. Quite appealing with her dark wavy hair and eyes that seem to capture and reflect the sunlight. Utterly extraordinary, really, in so many ways.

William says Jocelyn has decided to remain at the ranch through the summer, despite his quickly improving health. Amanda has invited her to join us for the two-week excursion into Yellowstone National Park next month. I rather hope she will do so.

Next week I intend to help the cowboys with the branding of cattle. Despite knowing I am a greenhorn in the eyes of these men, most much younger than I am, I hope to prove I am a help and not a hindrance.

Your brother,
Sebastian Whitcombe

Chapter Nine

The following Sunday morning, Jocelyn sat beside her brother in the double-seat spring wagon as William drove the team of horses toward Gibeon. Several of the cowboys were on horseback on either side of the wagon, all of them wearing their best hats in honor of the Sabbath, but it was Sebastian Whitcombe's presence on the back seat that Jocelyn was most aware of. A bothersome sensation, and one that happened frequently. Whenever he was near, she wanted him to be even closer. When he was absent, she found herself wondering where he was.

Behind her, above the creak of the wagon, the jangle of harness, and the clopping of horses' hooves, Sebastian asked, "How far is it into this town of yours?"

"About ten miles from the ranch house," William called back to him. "Takes us around an hour to get there in the wagon. Faster on horseback, if you're in a hurry."

"Amanda will be sorry she missed this first trip into town. She loves meeting new people."

Jocelyn glanced over her shoulder in time to see Sebastian lean back, his gaze taking in the passing countryside, a wide smile on his mouth. Did all future earls take this much pleasure in a wagon ride into town? She doubted it.

She twisted more on the seat. "Where do you attend church?"

"We have our own chapel on Hooke Manor. When I am in London, I worship at St. James's Church. It's quite near my London residence."

"And the earl and your sister?"

"Our father has a separate London house. But it is not far from mine. My father and Amanda also attend St. James's when they are in town for the season." He leaned forward a second time. "And you, Miss Overstreet? Where do you go to church when you are in New York?"

"Trinity Church."

He gave his head a slight shake. "I'm not familiar with it."

"It's the oldest Episcopal church in the city."

"I'm afraid I know little about New York City or its churches."

"Don't apologize, Mr. Whitcombe. I know even less about London." She looked at her brother as she faced forward once again. "If not for William's letters home, I would know nothing of it at all. Perhaps while you're at the ranch, you will enlighten me."

The remainder of the ride into town passed in silence. When they reached Gibeon, William steered the wagon to the side of the church on the east end of town. Sebastian hopped down as soon as the wheels stopped rolling and offered his hand to help Jocelyn descend. After drawing a breath, she placed her gloved fingers into his open palm. And as her feet touched the ground, he immediately tucked her hand into the crook of his arm.

Fluttery sensations flowed through her. Another bothersome reaction. What was wrong with her?

"Jocelyn Overstreet, as I live and breathe! Is that really you?"

She turned in the direction of the excited voice. "It is, indeed, Mrs. Hathaway."

Margaret Hathaway bustled forward. "It's been a coon's age since we've seen you in Gibeon."

"Six years to be precise." She smiled at the other woman a moment before embracing her. She'd always been fond of this bubbly, round-faced woman.

Margaret's gaze went to Sebastian. "And who is your young man here?"

She felt heat rise in her cheeks and quickly released her hold on his arm. "He isn't—" She broke off, swallowed, then continued, "Mr. Whitcombe, may I introduce Margaret Hathaway. She and her husband own the Teton General Store in Gibeon."

"Sebastian Whitcombe, at your service." He bowed with the sweep of an arm. "It is my great pleasure to meet you, madam."

Margaret's eyes widened. "Goodness gracious.

Listen to you. You're not from around these parts, that's for certain."

"Mr. Whitcombe is from England," Jocelyn said. "He and William went to school together."

"That was a mighty long time ago."

William moved to Sebastian's side. "It certainly was a long time, Mrs. Hathaway." Braced by his crutches, he leaned toward the woman. "Did he mention he's a viscount, son to the Earl of Hooke?"

Internally, Jocelyn winced. Why was her brother bragging about Sebastian being a member of the British aristocracy? And to Margaret Hathaway, of all people. She would, in turn, tell everyone when they visited the general store.

But Margaret didn't wait to spread the news in her store. She turned and called over her shoulder, "Harry, come here and meet Jocelyn Overstreet's young man. He's some kind of royalty."

Jocelyn's cheeks grew warm a second time as many heads turned in their direction.

Harry Hathaway, tall and beanpole thin, hurried toward his wife. "Yes, dear." He pushed at the bridge of his glasses, sliding them up his long nose. Then, his eyes now on Jocelyn, he said, "It's right good to see you again, Miss Overstreet. Been too long. Much too long." Another shift of his gaze. "And William, we heard about you and that buffalo. Fool thing to do, get between one of them beasts and whatever it wanted."

"I agree," William answered. "A fool thing to do."

Margaret elbowed her husband. "Harry, this is Mr.

Whitcombe. Got hisself some sort of title. What was it?" She peered up at Sebastian.

"Viscount, madam. Viscount Willowthorpe."

"I thought you said Whit something."

"I did. Whitcombe. But the title is not the same as my family name."

Margaret blinked a couple of times and a furrow formed on the bridge of her nose. "Sorry, young man. I'm confused. What's your full name and title and all?"

"Sebastian Leopold Edward Whitcombe, Viscount Willowthorpe." Again, he gave her a bow. "At your service."

"Good gracious." Margaret drew back from him. "I'm thankful we don't have to put up with that nonsense around here."

The heat in Jocelyn's cheeks intensified.

But Sebastian laughed. "I quite agree with you, madam. It feels very much like nonsense in your wonderful country."

Being mistaken for Jocelyn Overstreet's "young man" delighted Sebastian more than it should. And with the delight came, once again, the notion of Jocelyn accompanying him home to England. The image of him introducing her to the earl as his intended. Only this time, it didn't seem as preposterous as when he'd imagined it before. Why was that? Because he'd known her a few more days? Because they'd shared a few more conversations over evening meals? Because they'd shot that grizzly bear? Or because she'd blushed when the older woman suggested he and Jocelyn were more to each other than they were?

He returned his gaze to Margaret Hathaway. "Meeting you has been a pleasure, madam, but I believe it is time we all went inside." He offered his arm to Jocelyn again and was pleased when she accepted without hesitation. Then he walked with her toward the entrance of the white clapboard church, William on his crutches in their wake.

At the door, they met Reverend Truman Blankenship, a young man who didn't look old enough to shave, let alone to shepherd a congregation in the ways of the Lord. At Hooke Manor, the vicar was in his mid-seventies, his thick hair pure white, the loose skin of his neck resembling a turkey gobbler's. But to Sebastian the difference in those men's ages also seemed to represent their countries. England was old. Centuries upon centuries old. The American West was young. Fifty years ago, this town hadn't existed. Of course, eventually Reverend Blankenship might look as if he needed a shave, but hopefully this wild American West would persist even longer than that.

With that thought making him smile, he settled into a pew, William on the aisle with Jocelyn between her brother and him and three of the Eden's Gate cowboys on his right.

The next hour and a half passed pleasantly. The church pianist played with enthusiasm, and the congregation sang energetically, if not always on key. The good reverend might look young, but he was an excellent speaker and proclaimed the word of God with authority. His sermon on the prodigal son and the father who ran to meet him touched Sebastian's heart and caused him to think of the parable in a fresh way.

Would his own father welcome him back if he were to thwart the earl's expectations once again? Sebastian wasn't sure. The earl hadn't been happy with him for refusing to become engaged to Eliza Southwick. His father had wanted that union for a number of reasons, not the least of which was the stallion, Glenhaven, that would have come with Eliza into marriage. In the end, Eliza had chosen to marry Adam, Sebastian's illegitimate half-brother, thereby making Glenhaven a part of the stables at Hooke Manor in a different way. Eliza's generosity had helped Sebastian win his father's forgiveness. That time.

But if he defied the earl yet again, it was unlikely forgiveness would be granted.

The congregation rose for the closing hymn, *A Mighty Fortress is Our God.* Joy warmed Sebastian's heart as he joined in. The hymn had been a favorite of his mother's. The countess had often played it on the Steinway grand in the music room. If he closed his eyes, he could almost hear her soprano voice singing the words.

Another beautiful feminine voice caught his attention. It belonged to Jocelyn Overstreet. He stopped singing and looked her way. Her eyes were closed, and the expression on her face convinced him she meant each and every word of the hymn.

"'Dost ask who that may be? Christ Jesus, it is He;

Lord Sabaoth His name, from age to age the same, and He must win the battle.'"

The lyrics stirred Sebastian's heart, as if hearing them for the first time. He was not a man given to wild imaginings, but in that moment, he felt his mother smile down upon him, blessing the decisions he'd yet to make.

Chapter Ten

On the following Wednesday morning, Jocelyn sat on the dressing stool in her bedroom, tying the end of her braid with a ribbon.

Near the door to the bedroom, Mrs. Adler said, "It's going to be a hot day." Her disapproval was evident. Not of the weather but of Jocelyn's plans.

"It's usually hot at branding time."

"The branding's happening later than usual because of Mr. William. He wanted to be there. That means it'll be hotter than usual too." The housekeeper *tsked, tsked*.

Jocelyn fought to keep herself from smiling.

"Mr. William shouldn't be sitting on a horse yet, if you ask me. You ought to both stay put and let the men do the work they were hired to do."

That was the real problem, Jocelyn supposed. William hadn't asked Mrs. Adler's opinion. He'd decided on his own what he was going to do and when he was going to do it. Jocelyn had done the same. "Billy will be fine, Mrs. Adler. I'll make sure he doesn't overdo."

"You shouldn't be out there at all. It was one thing when you were a girl, but now you're a grown woman. You should act like it. Branding's no place for you."

"I was eight the first year I helped with branding, and I don't plan to miss the fun now."

"Fun. Hmm." Mrs. Adler crossed her arms over her chest and jerked her chin for emphasis. "Don't know what your mother was thinking, letting you take part in such a thing."

"Mama thought I should enjoy my summers on the ranch. That's what she was thinking."

"Enjoy?" Mrs. Adler's eyebrows rose. "Out there with men saying heaven knows what. The horses. The irons. Sweating. Getting so dirty it turns the bathtub to a mud pit."

Jocelyn laughed before giving the older woman a quick peck on the cheek. "I love you, Mrs. Adler, but you will never understand what it's like and why I love it."

"No, I won't." She sounded somewhat mollified. The kiss, it seemed, had done its work.

"Now, I'd better hurry. I don't want to get in trouble with the boss." Jocelyn grabbed her hat and slapped it onto her head before hurrying out of her bedroom.

She wouldn't have confessed it to the housekeeper, but she'd looked forward to this day from the moment she made the decision to remain at the ranch for the summer. As clear as anything, she remembered her mother seated astride her favorite pinto gelding, smiling and shouting orders to the men.

Her father was part of the memory too, although he'd never looked anything like a cowboy. Papa had always been the eastern dude who loved his wife and therefore loved what she loved. And Mama had loved this ranch and the work that went on here. She'd looked lovely and every inch a lady when they were in New York City. But whenever they returned to the ranch, Mama had come fully to life again.

This morning, Jocelyn realized how very like her mother she'd become.

Bella had been saddled and stood tied to a rail near the barn, but no men were left in sight, not even Sebastian or William. All of them had ridden to the place where the branding would be done. She must hurry and catch up with them. She didn't want to miss a moment.

She swung into the saddle, gathered the reins, and nudged Bella forward. In no time at all, the mare was cantering across the land, headed south. Well before she reached the site, Jocelyn saw the thick cloud of dust raised by the cows and calves moving closer to their destination.

She slowed the horse from canter to trot to walk, wanting to savor the moment. The morning air remained cool, and she felt certain she could smell the green of the grasses growing all around her. The soft mooing of cattle carried to her on the breeze. Soon enough, the bawls of calves would be heard above all else.

As Jocelyn and Bella got closer to the circle of cattle, one of the cowboys broke away and rode toward her. Only it wasn't one of the cowboys. It was Sebastian. The past couple of weeks had taken the newness out of his hat, boots, and denim trousers. The way he sat in the saddle had changed as well. He rode more like a seasoned cowpoke than an English gentleman.

And he looks good. Her heart stuttered at the thought.

He called out as he rode toward her. "William wondered if you'd changed your mind."

"Never." She smiled.

He reined his mount to a stop. "What is it you intend to do?"

"Rope some calves, I hope. Although I'm out of practice. Not much call for roping in New York."

He laughed with her. "I've always liked to learn new things, and your brother's promised to teach me to lasso a calf when he is more himself. But today I expect I'll learn what I need to do by observing."

"I'm surprised how well you fit in on the ranch."

His eyebrows rose. "Why surprising?"

"I may not have been to England, Mr. Whitcombe, but I'm fairly certain life as the heir to an earldom has little in common with life on a cattle ranch."

Sebastian watched her in silence for what seemed a long while before he said, "You are correct about that. Quite different."

"Tell me about it." She nudged Bella with her heels to move them toward the herd.

"I am not sure what to tell you or where to start."

The strength of her desire to know more about him,

about the way he lived his life, surprised her. "Start anywhere. Tell me how you spend your days."

"My half-brother, Adam, manages Hooke Manor. He informs me or my father if there is something we need to know about the tenants, the crops, the horses, and so forth. As a member of the peerage, I'm expected to stay current with politics, of course. Depending upon the time of year, I might go riding or hunting or fishing with friends during the day. We often entertain in the evenings, although that happens more frequently in town than at the manor."

Jocelyn glanced over at him, trying to imagine him in his world.

"I've traveled extensively on the Continent in recent years—Italy and France and Greece. I've been to Egypt with friends. Fascinating place, that. I daresay you would find it the same."

I daresay I would. "Papa planned to take us all to Europe for my fifteenth birthday. We were to stop in England first as William's schooling would have ended by then. Then the four of us were to travel around Europe for a couple of months before we all sailed home together. But then Mama sickened and died, and Papa lost all interest in traveling." She paused, the memories squeezing her heart. But this wasn't a day for sadness, so she shook off the memories. "As you may know, William hated sailing. He never got his sea legs. Just the sight of a ship made him queasy. That's one reason he rarely came home for visits during those years he was at Eton College. So once he was finished, he was determined never to travel to England or the Continent for any reason."

Sebastian nodded. "I suspected as much. About his seasickness, I mean. The poor boy was definitely homesick, but he stayed at the college during most breaks." He tipped his head slightly to one side as he looked at her. "Do you get seasick?"

"No." She grinned. "Father had a sailboat that we took out when we visited Newport in the summer. I've always loved the ocean."

"Then if you love the ocean, there's nothing to keep you from traveling to England and Europe."

She felt a familiar twinge of envy but pushed it away, as she always had. It seemed wrong to want something that had never happened because of Mama's death. Better not to think about it.

THAT MORNING WAS like nothing Sebastian had experienced before. He wasn't a stranger to hard work, but this was different. The noise. The dust. The smells. The heat. Since he was worthless with a rope, he'd volunteered to help wrestle the calves to the ground after they'd been lassoed. With the cow complaining not far off and the calf bawling in fear, he held the young animal steady while the hot iron was burned into its coat.

Sometime close to noon, William shouted above the din. "All right, men. Chuck's here with our lunch. Take a break."

Sebastian released the just-branded calf and stepped back as it bounded away. Sweat dripped off his forehead and down his spine. He pulled the kerchief from his back pocket and mopped his face. What he wouldn't give for a dip in the creek that cut right through the middle of Eden's Gate.

The men on horseback dismounted near the wagon that Chuck had driven to the site. Sebastian watched Jocelyn do the same, laughing at something the cook said. Dirt smudged one of her cheeks, and her hair curled wildly around her face, much of it having pulled free of the braid that hung over one shoulder. She had to be as hot and tired as the rest of them, but despite that, she looked beautiful.

When she glanced his way, the breath caught in his chest. What was this emotion flaring to life? Did he dare put a name to it? He admired her intelligence. He enjoyed her company. He'd played with the idea of introducing her to his father. Now, however, when he imagined her with him in England, it felt real, possible, desirable.

William interrupted his thoughts. "Sebastian! Get over here before the grub's all gone."

That broke the spell that had fallen over him. *Spell?* He almost scoffed aloud. He didn't believe in such things. Not of the magical type and certainly not of the romantic type. His parents' arranged marriage had been a good one, and he'd hoped to follow their example. No magic. Simply a good union resulting from a negotiated marriage contract between like-minded folk.

Jocelyn moved toward him, a plate in each hand. "Aren't you hungry?"

"As a matter of fact, I am."

"Good. This one is yours."

He took the plate she held out toward him.

She withdrew a fork from her shirt pocket. "You'll need this."

The thick stew on the plate—potatoes, carrots, onions, and beef covered in a brown gravy, along with a chunk of fresh bread—was more delicious than Sebastian expected, and conversation was non-existent until the last bit of food was scraped from the last plate in the circle.

"Mighty good, Chuck," Rocky said as he rose from the log that had served as a bench for three of the cowboys.

More praise was spoken as plates were carried to the wagon and stacked in a wash tub.

"Tom," Jake said, "stoke the fire. We've got another couple hundred calves to brand before we're done for the day."

Two hundred more? Sebastian grimaced even as he determined to get back to it. Perhaps he had something to prove to himself. His brief talk with Jocelyn that morning had made him ever more aware of the easy life he led compared to most others. In America, even wealthy men worked hard.

William limped to where Sebastian sat. "Want to try cutting calves out from the herd?"

"I'm unable to lasso them."

His friend chuckled. "I know that. But Jocelyn

managed to get her roping arm back this morning. The two of you can partner. You and your horse will cut the calf away from the other cows so Jocelyn can lasso it."

"Well then—" He looked in Jocelyn's direction— "I guess that's what we'll do."

"Don't worry," William added. "Goldrush will do the bulk of the work. You just need to point him at the calf you want and hang on tight, because he's gonna change directions faster than you think he will." With a tug on the brim of his hat, he walked away.

Chapter Eleven

As Jocelyn slowly settled herself on a chair in the dining room the next morning, William burst into laughter.

"Don't you dare, brother." She tried not to wince a second time.

"Afraid I can't help it, sister dear."

She narrowed her gaze at him. "You are not long out of your bed with a serious injury. I could see you right back into it with a different injury."

"Perhaps, but not today. Today I could outrun you."

Her muscles screamed that William was right. Even with a limp, he would be able to move faster than she could.

A sound drew her eyes to the entrance of the dining room in time to see Sebastian grimace as he moved toward a chair. Like her brother before her, she laughed. Hand over her mouth, she said, "I'm not alone in my aches and pains."

"I rather wish you were, Miss Overstreet." He sat.

"Not that I regret taking part in the branding yesterday. William, my respect for what you and your men do has increased enormously. Your letters made the ranch and the area sound exciting, but I fear I romanticized it all. I never imagined what you must do to maintain the ranch day in and day out. And I can tell, despite your injury, that you work every bit as hard as the men you employ."

William replied, "I've never seen you shirk work, Sebastian."

"No, but it isn't the same." He spooned scrambled eggs onto his plate. "My father is a careful man, and he has employed careful men to serve as his various estate managers. Because of it, the Whitcombe legacy is financially secure. I'm grateful for that." He lifted his gaze. "Hooke Manor is the largest of our estates and the family's main residence. Most of the land is leased to tenant farmers who grow crops and raise livestock like pigs and cows. There are demands that come with owning the land, of course, but nothing like it is here on Eden's Gate."

Jocelyn thought back to her conversation with Sebastian the previous day and wondered if he was content in the life he lived.

William's voice drew her from the brief reverie. "I was invited to visit Hooke Manor more than once when I was in England, but I never managed to make it happen. I'm sorry for that now." Looking at Sebastian, he added, "But you did manage to get me to the earl's London house. I even attended a couple of balls there before I returned to America for good."

"I can't quite picture you at a fancy dress ball," Jocelyn said as she spread jam on a muffin.

"Neither can I." Her brother laughed. "And I was there."

Sebastian gave his head a slow shake. "It is a world away from this one."

Once again she wondered if he was content with his role in life, and she asked, "Would you give up your world for one like this?"

The look on his face answered the question even before the words left his mouth. "No. I have a responsibility to my family and to the people who live on our lands. I would never turn my back on them. England and Hooke Manor are my destiny."

She couldn't explain the sudden emptiness she felt. Sebastian had only been at Eden's Gate for a month, and he'd stated his visit was for one year. And yet, she'd begun to envision him as a part of this ranch . . . and her there along with him. Which made no sense at all.

His place was in England. Her place was in New York. That's how it was meant to be.

AFTER WATCHING William and the cowboys mount their horses as if the previous day's exertions meant nothing to them, Sebastian walked to the creek and followed its winding path toward the east. For the first ten minutes, his sore muscles made him consider turning back. But he pressed on, and soon the mild exercise began to loosen the kinks and knots in his body. The morning air was mild, and the melody of the creek soothed him.

Jocelyn's question at the breakfast table had been unexpected. But it was his own swift and certain response that had surprised him more. As much as he'd fallen in love with this vast country, with those mountains ahead of him, with this ranch and the people on it, he wouldn't want to give up Hooke Manor and his life in England. Strange, wasn't it? For years, he'd resisted the idea of settling down, of marrying and providing the next heir for the Whitcombe legacy, of living the life he'd inherited rather than chosen. But when Jocelyn had asked the question, the answer had suddenly been there. No, he wouldn't give it up.

"But would she give up this?" he asked aloud, his gaze on the Tetons. "Would she give up New York and Overstreet Shipping?"

How he would love to talk to his brother right now. Adam had a good head on his shoulders, could look at situations and see them clearly, then find a solution. Adam had wanted to marry Eliza Southwick and against all odds he'd made it happen. Of course, it helped that Eliza had fallen completely in love with Adam, so much so she'd been willing to defy her father and disregard her social position to be with him.

"Would you give up your world for one like this?" He stopped walking as Jocelyn's question reverberated in his memory. He'd answered no to that question. His sister-in-law had answered yes to a similar one.

Am I wrong? Should I make a different choice?

No. The same certainty zinged through him. He

wasn't wrong. England was where he belonged. And Jocelyn was the woman he wanted to be there with him. That too came with certainty.

Now all he needed was to make her believe the same.

Dear Adam,

You may well be surprised to receive another letter so soon from me. Earlier today, when I was out walking, I wished I could talk to you. I could dearly use your advice but you are too far away. I shall have to work out my questions by myself.

You may find this hard to believe, but I have concluded I want Jocelyn Overstreet to be my future bride. The first problem, of course, is that she does not appear to want a husband. Certainly she does not need one. Unlike the young American heiresses who have found their way to England's shores in search of titled husbands, Miss Overstreet is content to remain independent. Independence does seem to be a hallmark of many American women. I shudder to think what an influence this will have on our dear sister who is already quite headstrong, as you know. This could be another strike against Americans in Father's eyes.

And speaking of Father, the second problem regarding Miss Overstreet is this. He will be quite opposed to such a union. I would be surprised if he hasn't compiled a list of possible brides from the daughters and granddaughters of his peers so he can parade them in front of me upon my return. A substantial dowry is not required, but he does expect a lady of quality to be the mother of his grandchildren. A <u>British</u> lady of quality. He has *never held the Americans in high regard, and he has had less than nice things to say about "the invasion" of American brides. He complains of them marrying into our finest families and bringing their "frontier ways" with them. More than once I have listened to him list them off, the women who have invaded our shores. And he complains about them, whether or not he has met them.*

I wonder now. Did it occur to Father that, during my year in America, I might meet a woman who would finally interest me in matrimony? I daresay not. He believes I am averse to marriage. Which is not true. I am averse to marriage to the <u>wrong</u> *woman.*

I do not need his permission to wed the woman of my choice, of course, but I would not want to bring a bride into a hostile environment. Nor would I wish to live estranged from Father until he softens or dies. And I fear he would never soften.

For now, I will concentrate on solving the first problem I named above. The second problem doesn't exist if she does not wish to marry.

Still, if you—having some experience in the matter—think of a solution to the second problem, I would be glad to hear it.

Your brother,

Sebastian Whitcombe

Chapter Twelve

The first day of July brought high temperatures with it. Even the hum of bees around the flower bushes Mrs. Adler tended with diligence seemed weakened by the heat in late afternoon.

Jocelyn was brushing a yearling colt in the shade of the barn when a cloud of dust in the distance alerted her to the approach of a wagon. She stepped away from the barn, squinting for a better look.

"Wonder who that is," William said as he joined her.

"Whoever it is, they're in a hurry to get here."

"Not coming from town. Could be somebody got injured, and we're the closest place to get help." He went to his horse and mounted it. "I'd better find out." With a nudge of his heels, he rode out of the barnyard.

The dust from William's horse's hooves hadn't yet settled when Sebastian appeared on Jocelyn's other side. "Is something amiss?"

"I'm not sure." Although the sun was at her back,

115

she shielded her eyes, as if that would make it easier to see who was driving hard toward the ranch house.

"It's a coach," Sebastian said after an extended silence.

Jocelyn watched as William met the vehicle. The coach stopped, and she assumed her brother and the driver exchanged information. Then it started moving again, traveling slower now, William's horse cantering along beside the coach.

"Doesn't look as if there is need for alarm." Sebastian took a step back, as if to return to whatever he'd been doing.

At the same time, Jocelyn took a step forward. "There's a horse tied to the back of the coach. Sebastian, look. I think it's one of those Palouse horses."

He returned to her side. "I do believe you're right. You don't suppose that's my sister and Roger, do you?" He paused, then said, "I rather think it must be. And I should have known she would come back with a horse of her own."

A short while later, the coach rolled into the barnyard, and Amanda leaned out the window, smiling and waving at them. "Hello! Are you surprised to see us?"

"You should have let us know you were returning today." Sebastian moved to open the door for her.

Amanda took her brother's hand and let him help her to the ground, Roger disembarking right behind her. Instead of releasing Sebastian's hand, Amanda pulled him toward the horse at the back of the coach. "Look at her. Isn't she wonderful?"

"Indeed. She is a beauty."

Jocelyn had to agree. The young mare—tall and sleek—had beautiful markings. She was midnight black everywhere except her rump, which had a blanket of white hair with black spots of varying sizes spread around it.

Amanda untied the rope and led the mare away from the coach and into the shade beside the yearling. Sebastian followed his sister there.

"We kept a rather slow pace most of the day," Amanda said. "Until the ranch came into view. Then I told the coachman to ask the horses for more speed. I couldn't wait to get here."

William tied his saddle horse to the hitching rail before joining Jocelyn and Roger, all of them examining the mare.

"What are you calling her?" William asked.

"Ebony."

Jocelyn nodded. "I like that."

"I came up with it," Roger interjected.

Amanda laughed. "It's true. He did."

"And do you plan to take her with us to England?" Sebastian stroked the mare's head.

"Of course I do. If the horses in Buffalo Bill's show can handle a week aboard a ship crossing the Atlantic, so can Ebony." Amanda ran a hand over the mare's sweat-dampened coat. "With Eliza and Adam's permission, I'd like to breed her with Glenhaven. Imagine Ebony's coloring with Glenhaven's conformation and speed. Imagine a Palouse horse in the Grand National."

Sebastian leaned to the side to look at his sister. "Aren't you getting a little ahead of yourself?"

Amanda laughed again. "Perhaps. But there is nothing wrong with having dreams for the future."

Jocelyn smiled. She loved listening to these two banter. They had such an easy manner when together, despite the ten years that separated them.

"Are you hungry?" William looked between Amanda and Roger. "I could have Chuck prepare something for you. We've still got over three hours to wait for supper. Most of the boys are on the south range, so we planned to eat a little later than usual."

"I don't need to eat," Amanda answered. "But I could use a bath." She brushed at her skirt, raising a small dust cloud from it. "See?"

Jocelyn turned from the horses. "Come with me, Amanda. I'm sure we can have a bath ready for you in no time at all."

AFTER WATCHING his sister and Jocelyn walk away, Sebastian turned his attention once more to the spotted mare. "Amanda has an eye for horses. She's a lot like Adam in that regard."

Roger removed his hat and raked his hair with the fingers of one hand. "She wanted to buy more than just one horse, but I talked her out of it."

"Then bully for you. We don't need to take an entire herd of Palouse horses back to England." He glanced at William. "Not to mention what our host might think of it."

William grinned. "I have no problem with more

horses in our corrals and paddocks. Although the horses on this ranch are here to work, just like the cowboys." He turned. "And speaking of work, I need to get to mine." He walked away.

Sebastian turned his full attention on Roger. "I appreciate you bringing Amanda back, safe and sound."

"To be honest, I was rather glad to see some more of the country. And while Amanda was off with Mr. and Mrs. Crawford, looking over the herd and deciding which one to buy, I was able to do lots of sketches. Landscapes, horses, and every man who works on the Crawford ranch. Gave me a great opportunity to talk with them. Quite the stories some had to tell. One of the older men used to drive cattle up from Texas. Harrowing experiences with lightning storms and stampedes, horse thieves, and more. You would have enjoyed listening to him."

"I'm sure I would have. I am beginning to wish I'd accompanied Amanda myself."

"But look at you." Roger took a step backward and appraised Sebastian with that artist's eye of his. "You look like you've become one of the cowboys. Just the way you wanted."

Sebastian chuckled. "I've tried my best, but I believe the men still think me something of an oddity."

"Old chum, you are deemed something of an oddity in England as well."

"What?"

"You've managed to avoid marriage to some of the most beautiful and wealthy young women in London every season since you left school. Young women who were obviously smitten with you and willing to become the future Countess of Hooke, need I add. And if that wasn't enough, you chose to spend a year in the American wilderness rather than socializing with the cream of British society. Your fascination with this country baffles many of your peers and especially your father."

"True enough."

In unspoken agreement, the two men turned away from Ebony and the yearling beside her and walked toward the house.

"I'm grateful to have you for a friend, Sebastian." Roger chuckled softly. "Another reason many think you are odd. Your choice of friends. William Overstreet. Adam. Me."

Sebastian laughed as he nodded. "Who am I to argue?"

They continued into the house. While Roger climbed the stairs to wash up, Sebastian went into the parlor, his thoughts lingering on his friend's last words.

It was true. Their friendship was unusual. Roger, the son of a London merchant, hadn't been educated at Eton and Cambridge. In fact, he and Sebastian had met one night in a narrow dark street in London. Sebastian and a few of his university mates had been on their way to a private house party when they came upon three thieves in the process of relieving another man of his valuables while beating on him for sport. But the thieves had run away as soon as it was clear they were outnumbered.

"I say." Sebastian had knelt beside the victim of the assault. "Are you all right?"

"I will be." The man groaned. "I think."

Sebastian offered an arm to help him up from the ground. "May we be of any assistance?"

"You already have been." His face was beginning to show signs of bruising. He winced as he touched his cheek. "Roger Bernhardt is my name."

"Sebastian Whitcombe."

"Well, sir, I am obliged to you. I should have been paying more attention to my surroundings."

"Let's go, Whitcombe," one of Sebastian's classmates, Lester Pritchett, said. "The ladies are waiting for us."

Bertie Phillips laughed. "No lady waits for you, Pritchett, and well you know it."

Sebastian didn't know why he'd done it—Roger Bernhardt didn't appear seriously injured—but he turned to the others. "Go on without me. I'll join you soon. I want to be sure Mr. Bernhardt gets home safely."

That had been the start of their friendship, and they'd remained close ever since.

"Another reason many think you are odd. Your choice of friends."

He'd never thought about it that way, but Roger was right. Sebastian's closest friendships were—and had been from a young age—with those who weren't quite accepted by those of his own class.

He supposed that did make him odd. And perhaps it also explained his interest in a certain American miss.

Chapter Thirteen

Sebastian spent each day of the following week doing whatever work was called for. He rose early, ate breakfast, and rode out with the men. He returned for supper, hot and sweaty and weary to the bone. He mended fences. He helped rescue a calf from a bog. He practiced his roping, which remained pathetic—in everyone's opinion, although he was the only one who said so. He put a couple of green broke horses through their paces. He moved cattle from one part of the range to another.

Eager for the trip into Yellowstone National Park, Roger decided to head up to Gardiner, Montana a couple of days ahead of Sebastian and Amanda. Jocelyn, to Sebastian's great disappointment, had decided not to join the small party.

With plenty of paint supplies in Roger's possession —more important to him than food or clothing—he set off in a wagon with Rocky Turner for company, calling back to Sebastian and Amanda that he would see them soon.

But plans changed unexpectedly.

On the next Monday morning, the day the Whitcombe siblings were to begin the trip north to Gardiner to meet with Roger, a knock sounded on Sebastian's bedroom door as he finished dressing. Surprised to have an early visitor, he moved to answer it at once and found the housekeeper on the other side.

"Mrs. Adler?"

"It's your sister, Mr. Whitcombe." She glanced down the hall. "She's not well. She's not well at all."

He brushed past her and rushed to Amanda's room. Stepping inside, he saw Jocelyn seated on a chair beside the bed, placing a cloth on his sister's forehead.

"What's wrong?" he asked as he drew near.

"She has a fever."

Amanda rolled her head from side to side and muttered something unintelligible. Her skin looked blotchy, and a sheen of perspiration on her upper lip caught the light from the lamp on the nightstand.

"How long has she been like this?"

Jocelyn answered, "I don't know. I came to ask her something. I knew she'd be up since you two were planning to leave right after breakfast. When she didn't answer my knock, I . . . I opened the door and found her like this."

From behind Sebastian, Mrs. Adler said, "I'll send someone for the doctor."

"Thank you, Mrs. Adler." Jocelyn leaned in and touched Amanda's cheek. "She's burning up. It must have come on suddenly in the night. She was fine at supper last night."

Dread tightened Sebastian's chest. If something were to happen to Amanda while they were in America, it would be his fault for acquiescing to her desire to come with him. He should have refused. He should have left her behind in England.

"And she was so looking forward to your excursion in the park," Jocelyn added softly.

Yellowstone. Those plans had been forgotten as soon as the housekeeper told him Amanda was sick. But Roger was waiting for them in Gardiner. He needed to be told.

Sebastian turned and went out of the room, calling to the housekeeper. "Mrs. Adler, wait." He went down the stairs two at a time. "Whoever goes for the doctor needs to send a telegram for me. I'll write it down."

The woman nodded, hesitated, then patted his hand. "Don't you worry, Mr. Whitcombe. Your sister will be fine. Dr. Grant will see to it."

He wanted to believe her. But he'd seen people sicken and die, despite the ministrations of well-educated, well-meaning physicians.

God in Heaven, protect Amanda. Heal her, Lord, I beseech You.

As if he'd prayed the words aloud, the housekeeper nodded again. "The good Lord's with her. You can be sure of it." She took a small step backward. "You write down your telegram, and I'll have one of the boys get his horse ready to ride to town for the doctor."

He felt a surge of gratitude, thankful the woman no

longer regarded him and Amanda as unwelcome intruders. Her concern for his sister was genuine. He saw it in her eyes.

Not long after—with the message to be telegraphed to a hotel in Gardiner, Montana written and placed in Tom Flores's shirt pocket before he rode off to town—Sebastian returned upstairs to his sister's bedside. He sat in a chair opposite Jocelyn and took hold of Amanda's left hand. She lay perfectly still now. Too still. Almost lifeless. He found it difficult to breathe as he watched her.

"Someone's ridden to town?" Jocelyn asked.

He nodded. "Tom volunteered."

Just then, the housekeeper entered the bedroom, carrying a pitcher of fresh water. "Miss Joss, you and Mr. Whitcombe should go down and eat something. I can see to the young miss." She rounded the bed to set the pitcher on the stand near Jocelyn's left elbow.

Jocelyn shook her head. "I'll stay. Thank you, Mrs. Adler."

"Then I'll bring a breakfast tray up to you. Won't do for you to go without eating." She left the room, saying, "Can't have you falling ill yourself."

Sebastian looked at Jocelyn. "Mrs. Adler may be right. I don't want you to get sick too. I can tend my sister."

"I assure you, Mr. Whitcombe, I am perfectly able to care for Amanda until Dr. Grant arrives. I won't starve." She removed the cloth from Amanda's forehead and moistened it in a bowl with water from the pitcher. After wringing it out, she waved it in the air to cool it, folded it, and returned it to Amanda's forehead. Then she moistened a second cloth and wiped it across his sister's lips. Her gaze locked on her patient's face. "Amanda will be terribly disappointed about Yellowstone. She's talked of little else since returning from Washington."

"There'll be other opportunities."

"Not for long. Winter starts early in these parts. If you plan to return to England in May, the next two months is all you can count on for trips into the park. Most years, the snow keeps visitors away till the end of June."

"Then we'll make certain to visit it this summer. And hopefully, next time we plan to go, you'll accept our invitation to accompany us. Perhaps a shorter excursion will be in order."

After that, they fell into silence, the only sound in the room his sister's shallow breathing.

JOCELYN COULDN'T HAVE EXPLAINED to Sebastian or anyone else why she felt such a strong need to remain at Amanda's bedside. While she'd expected Lady Amanda Whitcombe, daughter of an English earl, to be puffed up and full of her own importance, almost from the start she'd found the young woman to be warm and lively and refreshing to be with. But it was something more than simply liking Amanda that kept Jocelyn nearby. A need she couldn't name.

Mrs. Adler brought the promised breakfast tray, and

later, the housekeeper came to carry it back to the kitchen, unhappy with how little had been eaten. The clock in the hall ticked off the minutes. More loudly than usual, it seemed. Jocelyn moistened cloths, left them on the young woman's forehead until the heat from her body dried them, then replaced the dry cloth with another damp one.

At last, Sebastian rose. "Since there is nothing for me to do . . ." He let the words fade into silence.

Jocelyn looked up. "Yes. Do go. There truly isn't anything you can do for her."

He frowned, nodded, then left the room.

Not long after, William rapped lightly on the door-jamb. "How is she?" he asked in a low voice.

"Not good. I keep thinking her fever will break, but it doesn't."

He moved a couple of steps into the room, his limp less noticeable than it had been a week ago. "I'll pray she bounces back fast. No fun to be trapped in a sickbed. But at least she's got a good nurse in you. I can attest to that."

Jocelyn nodded but didn't reply. Soon after, William departed, much as Sebastian before him.

The sun had climbed close to its zenith by the time Dr. Grant appeared in the bedroom doorway, a worn black leather bag in hand. "How is the girl?" He approached the bed.

"A little quieter now. But her fever remains high."

After setting his bag on the empty chair beside the bed, he opened it and withdrew a stethoscope. "Has she spoken to you?"

"No. She mumbles from time to time, but she doesn't seem aware that I'm here."

"Mrs. Adler says you've taken good care of her."

"I've done little. Just tried to bring down her temperature."

He pressed the end of his stethoscope to Amanda's chest. "That is important, my dear. Don't think otherwise."

While the doctor examined his patient, Jocelyn rose and walked to the window, arching her back and stretching her arms and torso. Beyond the glass, she saw a couple of men ride away from the barn.

A memory swooped in. Two other men galloping horses away from the barn, one riding hell-bent-for-leather toward town to get the doctor, the other racing to find her father on the eastern range. On that day, it had been her mother who lay in the bed, her breathing shallow, her face pale and dotted with perspiration, the room gripped in a terrible silence. Jocelyn had been thirteen, on her way to becoming a woman while still remaining a child. She'd been terrified and had run from the room and hidden herself in the shadows of her father's study.

Her mother hadn't died that day, but she'd never returned to good health either. Jocelyn had dreaded visiting Mama's room, seeing her fade a little more each day. So Jocelyn had often stayed away. With each passing week, she'd spent less and less time beside her mother's bed. And then, one day, God had taken Mama home to heaven, and it had been too late to sit with her, to comfort her, to share stories and secrets, to ask questions that might help Jocelyn in the future.

Tears blurred her vision. "Doctor, please excuse me," she whispered.

Sounding distracted, he answered, "Of course."

She slipped from the room, went down the stairs and out the door. On the front porch, she sank onto a chair, eyes closed, feeling a pain in her chest that threatened to crush her. How long had it been since she'd remembered that terrible year, a terrible year that began with her mother's fever?

"Miss Overstreet?"

Sucking in a breath, she opened her eyes to find Sebastian on the other side of the porch railing.

"Is it . . . What has—" He stopped abruptly, his gaze shooting to the front door. His face paled.

"The doctor is with her now. I . . . I'm sure he will talk to you soon."

He released a breath. "When I saw you, sitting there, I . . . I . . ." He let the words trail into silence.

"I'm sorry, Mr. Whitcombe," she said softly. "I didn't mean to alarm you. I was upset about something else."

Concern returned to his expression, but she understood the concern was now for her. Tears sprang to her eyes a second time.

"Miss Overstreet."

The way he said her name caused something comforting to swirl inside of her. How was that possible when only moments before she'd felt bereft? She motioned him away with her hand. "I'm fine. You should go in. Dr. Grant will want to speak with you."

He stared at her for what seemed a long while. Then, finally, he nodded, turned, and went to the front door.

Chapter Fourteen

Days later, on his way down to breakfast, Sebastian rapped on the doorjamb of Amanda's room. "May I come in?"

"Of course." His sister pushed herself up against the pillows at her back.

There was some color in her cheeks again, and her eyes had lost the glazed look that had worried him so much.

"Sebastian, I am ever so bored with doing nothing."

He settled onto the chair by the bed. "Perhaps the doctor will allow you out of bed for a short while today."

She opened her mouth, as if to protest, but she was interrupted by coughing. A sound from her lungs that made him cringe.

When the room silenced at last, he said, "And that cough is the reason you were told to remain in bed. It could be a sign of something more serious."

Amanda huffed. "I *don't* have pneumonia, if that's

what worries you. It's nothing but a cold. I haven't had even a hint of a fever for at least two days, and I am feeling much stronger. I do not need to be coddled. I need to be up and moving around. I need to *do* something."

"All the same—" He frowned at her— "you must obey Dr. Grant."

Eyes lowered to her folded hands, his sister drew in a slow breath.

To give herself time to think? To hold back another coughing fit? To calm her irritation with him and the doctor? Sebastian couldn't be sure.

After what seemed a long while, she looked at him. "All right, brother dear. I will do as I'm instructed. I shall obey the doctor." Her words dripped with sweetness.

He doubted the veracity of her promise but nodded anyway.

"I rather spoiled our plans for the next couple of weeks. I'm sorry for that. Did you hear from Roger?"

"Yes. He offered to return to the ranch, but I sent him word to go on with his trip into the park. You and I will try to go another time before the summer ends."

Amanda covered her mouth and coughed, the sound not quite as harsh as before but still troubling.

His sister flicked her fingers at him. "Go on with you. Have your breakfast. Go round up a cow or something. You've wasted enough time at my bedside this week. I will read a book or I will sleep. If I must stay in bed to keep you happy, I don't need you here to watch me do it."

"If you're sure." He rose from the chair.

She released a soft sigh. "I'm sure. Go on."

Sebastian leaned down to kiss her forehead, then made his escape. The truth, time spent in a sick room was torture to him. It had always been that way. The illness of another person left him feeling useless. Worse, sometimes it made him agitated, almost angry. He wanted to command the patient to rise, get out of bed, and walk, but not out of a heart of compassion. Much to his shame.

Still mulling that thought, he entered the dining room. Jocelyn was alone at the breakfast table, a plate of food untouched before her.

"Good morning," he said, drawing her gaze.

A smile played across her lips. "Good morning."

"William not down yet?" He walked to the sideboard.

"He's eaten already and gone. He has business in Pocatello."

"That's right. I forgot it was Friday." Sebastian filled a plate with food—eggs and sausages and pan fried bread—then went to sit opposite Jocelyn. "He asked me if I wanted to go with him, but I thought I should stay at the ranch."

"I don't believe Amanda needs you to sit with her any longer."

"Not only doesn't she need me with her. She doesn't *want* me with her." He speared a bite of eggs with his fork.

Jocelyn's laugh was light and airy. "She said as much

about my company before I came downstairs. I'd say she is out of danger."

Sebastian watched as Jocelyn spread a dark red jam on a slice of fried bread, and suddenly he was aware of how deserted the house felt. Chuck wasn't banging around in the kitchen. Whatever had the housekeeper's attention, it too was a silent endeavor. William was at this moment riding south toward Pocatello, and whatever their chores this morning, the rest of the Eden's Gate cowboys weren't anywhere close to the house.

"So how will you occupy your time today," Jocelyn asked, "now that Amanda has no need of you?"

"I'm not sure. What about you?"

She took a sip of water from a glass. "Today I get serious about putting William's office in order."

Sebastian lifted his eyebrows, inviting more information.

"My brother's record keeping is abysmal. One reason I chose to stay for the entire summer was to reorganize his account books and help make sure the ranch's finances are tracked more efficiently. I've put it off, but I can't delay any longer. The summer is half over already."

"Could I be of help?"

"I doubt Billy's stuffy office is where you want to spend your day, Mr. Whitcombe."

"You're wrong, Jocelyn. I would like it very much, as long as it meant spending the day with you." Sebastian hadn't planned to say what he did. But he didn't want to take it back. Not any of it.

JOCELYN'S PULSE had quickened at the sound of her given name on his lips. Was he aware that he'd used it? She couldn't be sure.

"Please," he added softly. "Allow me to be of service."

Her heart—for some unknown reason—longed to say yes, but instead, she answered, "But you enjoy being on the range with the other men."

"True." He leaned forward. "But I also enjoy the time I spend with you."

And I, you.

"My penmanship is rather fine, Miss Overstreet."

She bit back the urge to tell him to call her Jocelyn once more.

"You won't regret making me your clerk. I promise." He smiled.

Something warm curled in her belly in response. Almost as if he'd promised more than to be a good clerk.

Whatever is wrong with me?

Sebastian slid his chair away from the table. "When do we begin?"

"I suppose there is no time like the present."

His smile broadened. "Agreed."

He stood, came around the table, and placed his hands on the back of her chair. She glanced up and over her shoulder at him, then rose as he pulled the chair back from the table. She wouldn't have been surprised if he'd offered his hand, as if to escort her onto the dance floor.

Warmth climbed in her cheeks. Where on earth would her fanciful thoughts take her next? She needed to plant her feet firmly on the floor again. Or at least put a little distance between herself and Sebastian.

She stepped away from the table. "I will meet you in the office in a few minutes." Then she hurried from the dining room and up the stairs. Once in her bedroom, she sank onto the side of the bed. Hands on her still-warm cheeks, she forced herself to breathe slowly, hoping it would force her heart to do the same.

What had just transpired? Why did it feel as if something significant had changed between her and Sebastian? He'd entered the dining room. He'd asked about her plans for the day. He'd offered to help her. And then he'd called her by name.

"You're wrong, Jocelyn. I would like it very much, as long as it meant spending the day with you." Her heart hiccuped as his words repeated in her memory.

She'd learned to enjoy Sebastian's company in the weeks since his arrival at Eden's Gate. She'd come to like many things about him—the way he cared for his sister and friends, his willingness to pitch in where needed, his work ethic, his good humor. But this . . . this feeling about him was something new. Something foreign. Something unexpected.

Her heart hiccuped a second time as she tried to put a name to what she felt. Admitting she liked Sebastian Whitcombe wasn't quite enough. This feeling seemed stronger than liking, stronger than friendship.

A strange buzzing sounded in her ears while the air seemed to leave the room.

No, it wasn't possible she felt anything more than friendship for Sebastian. Weeks ago, when she'd found herself imagining both of them staying on the ranch, she'd remembered that his place was in England and hers was in New York. That had put an end to useless daydreams. The situation hadn't changed since then.

And yet . . .

Closing her eyes, she gave her head a quick shake. She would think on this no more. There was work to do, and she'd best get on with it.

As she rose from the bed, she resisted the urge to check her reflection. Why should she look? She'd brushed her hair and forced the curls into submission upon arising. What more did she need to do? There was no one she needed to impress.

So why did her pulse quicken yet again when she recalled the way Sebastian had looked at her across the breakfast table? When she remembered the timbre of his voice when he spoke her name?

Merciful heavens! This could not continue.

———

SEBASTIAN STOOD in the middle of William's office, his gaze roaming the room. The walls were paneled with a dark wood, and floor-to-ceiling bookcases lined one full wall and half of another. The office's lone window on the north side of the house let in anemic light. The large desk was almost too big for the size of the room.

Between the dim light and the crowded conditions, the room felt claustrophobic. No wonder William would rather be out working with the men, rather than keeping the ranch accounts within these walls.

A sound from the hallway drew him around. A moment later, Jocelyn came through the doorway. Her gaze met his briefly, then lowered as she moved past him. She took a seat behind the desk before looking at him again.

"Shall we begin?" She pulled a ledger from a corner of the desk.

"Of course." He moved a chair around to one side of the desk, the window at his back. "Just tell me what you need me to do."

She flipped through a few pages of the book. Was she looking for information or avoiding meeting his gaze? He suspected the latter, and it made him smile. He'd known for some time that he wanted her to marry him, but he hadn't been sure how to convince her she wanted the same. Perhaps it wouldn't be as difficult as he'd feared. Perhaps he had cause to hope for a change of heart.

"Mr. Whitcombe?"

He blinked—and realized she'd asked a question before speaking his name. "Sorry," he said. "Woolgathering."

One of her brows cocked before she turned the chair toward the bookcase. Her fingers ran over the spines of numerous ledgers before she removed several from the shelf. Swiveling back to the desk, she set the books in front of Sebastian. "We must begin with inventory. We need an accurate accounting of cattle, horses, supplies. I wouldn't mind knowing the number of chickens in the coop or how many cats and dogs are in the barn. Everything and anything we can count should be counted."

"And that information is in these?" He opened the top ledger.

"It should be. But I doubt my brother has been thorough. For now, we will find as many details as possible. Inventory. Expenses. Income. Then we will go in search of whatever is not contained therein. Chuck will be able to help with all the food supplies. Jake Foster will help us with the livestock."

"And what information does William have?"

She sighed as she shook her head. "I don't know how things got away from him to this degree."

"The ranch is in financial trouble?"

"Mmm."

"How serious is it?"

She met his gaze, and he knew she was trying to decide how much to tell him. Of course, it wasn't any of his business. That much was true. She had every right to tell him nothing, despite his offer of help. But the fate of Eden's Gate mattered. To William. To Jocelyn. To everyone who lived and worked there. And it mattered to Sebastian.

"Jocelyn." He said her name softly, encouragingly.

"I'm not sure." She sighed a second time. "Serious enough that he took your rent money when you came to stay."

Sebastian sat back, feeling his eyes go wide.

"He would never have rented the house if he hadn't been desperate." A tentative smile curved the corners of her mouth, there and gone. "To you or to anyone else. You were always meant to be his guest, not a tenant."

"It was my idea to pay for our accommodations. I insisted. He never asked for money."

"Perhaps not, but he was more than glad to receive it once it was offered."

"I wish I'd known." Sebastian reached across the desk to touch the back of Jocelyn's hand.

Tears welled in her eyes as she whispered, "He kept it from me too. Even though I could have helped him."

Sebastian longed to draw Jocelyn into his arms, to let her rest her head on his shoulder while he whispered words of comfort. Would she welcome it? Did she need his offer of solace?

After a while, she sniffed and withdrew her hand. "We had better get started."

Chapter Fifteen

After a long day in William's office—bent over ledgers that said too much and too little at the same time—Jocelyn retreated to her bedroom to change. If she had her way, she would strip off her dress, drop onto the bed, and not budge until morning. But that wasn't an option. Mrs. Adler had announced dinner would be ready soon, and the housekeeper expected Jocelyn to be at the table. Sebastian expected to see her as well, and she wouldn't disappoint him. Not after everything he'd done for her today.

Only that wasn't the real reason she wouldn't stay in her room. She *wanted* to spend more time with Sebastian. Time when her attention wasn't focused on figures and letters written in her brother's unruly hand.

Unbidden, she remembered Sebastian's voice as he'd whispered, *"Jocelyn."*

Sebastian, her heart responded now.

Jocelyn could scarcely remember the last time she'd yearned to spend time in a particular gentleman's company. If ever. And of all men who could have awakened such feelings, did it have to be this Englishman whose life demanded he live an ocean away? A man she would never see again after she returned to New York.

O Lord, what am I to do with these feelings?

She waited, holding her breath, hoping for an answer. None came.

Half an hour later, after a quick sponge-bath, the tidying of her hair, and putting on a dark green dress—one of her favorites—she left her bedroom. Halfway down the stairs, she saw Sebastian standing at the large parlor windows. A soft creak from a step caused him to turn toward her. He didn't speak, but his eyes said he appreciated the effort she'd taken with her appearance. Silly that it mattered to her, but it did.

"Miss Joss." Mrs. Adler appeared in the dining room doorway. "There you are. Come along, the two of you. Your dinner's going to get cold."

Sebastian smiled as he approached the stairs, and Jocelyn's insides went all fluttery as he held out a hand to her. Not the first time he'd done so since his arrival at Eden's Gate. But for some reason, this time seemed different. More intimate.

"Will Amanda be joining us?" she asked.

"No. Mrs. Adler already took her a tray." He escorted her to her usual place, then rounded the table to take his seat opposite her. "Feels a little strange, doesn't it?"

"Strange?"

"Just the two of us once again."

"Yes. It does."

The housekeeper made a soft sound in her throat as she carried a platter of meat to the table and set it between them. Did she agree that having only the two people in the dining room was strange? Did she disapprove that Jocelyn had been alone with Sebastian all day? Or did the sound mean nothing at all?

"Thank you, Mrs. Adler," Jocelyn said.

The older woman set a bowl of peas and onions and another of boiled potatoes next to the meat platter. "You're welcome." She returned to the kitchen.

Sebastian leaned forward. "I do believe Mrs. Adler has warmed to me a little more."

"Do you?" Jocelyn shook her head.

"Am I mistaken?"

"Mrs. Adler is fiercely loyal to the Overstreets, especially to the son and daughter of Cynthia Munford Overstreet. She can also be overprotective of those *children*, which I'm sure you've noticed. She may not dislike you as much as she did upon your arrival, Mr. Whitcombe, but warmth may be asking too much of her."

"But since you like me, that improves my chances. Right?"

Happiness bubbled up inside her. "What makes you think I like you, sir?"

"How could you help it?" He straightened his shoulders and turned his profile toward her. First one side, then the other.

Jocelyn's happiness spilled over then, and she laughed.

He drew back, looking as if his feelings were hurt. "Do you deny that you like me?"

She sobered, and after several moments, whispered, "No, I do not deny it."

He didn't smile. He didn't speak. He simply looked at her, and the world shifted in response.

———

SEBASTIAN TRIED TO LOOK CALM—AND hoped he succeeded. But it was a facade. His heart raced. His gut tightened. His mouth was parched. And he felt a desire unlike anything he'd felt before. It was more than physical, although it was that as well. The only way he could describe the feeling was to call it *heart-hunger*. His heart hungered for Jocelyn. *He* hungered for Jocelyn.

Perhaps she read his thoughts, for color rose into her cheeks. She broke their locked gazes and looked down at her plate. The room seemed to hold its breath. He was drawn to his feet, as if by an invisible cord. As he rounded the end of the table for a second time this evening, he sensed her awareness of his movements even though she kept her eyes averted.

"Jocelyn." His hand fell lightly on her shoulder.

Now she looked at him.

"Jocelyn," he repeated, even softer than before.

Did he pull her up from her chair or did she rise of her own accord? Whatever the case, suddenly she stood before him. He lowered his head. She tipped hers back, her fingertips resting on his chest, as if to balance herself. Perhaps she rose on tiptoes to meet his lips. The kiss was light and tentative, but it caused emotions to explode within him.

After a long while, he drew back his head and watched as she opened her eyes, beautiful eyes filled with questions. He had questions of his own—about the wisdom of what he'd done and what he wanted to do.

"Why did you do that, Mr. Whitcombe?"

"Please call me Sebastian."

After a brief hesitation, she said, "Sebastian, why did you do that?"

"Because I have thought of little else today."

"Even as you read the ledgers?"

He smiled. "Even then."

"But why?"

"Because you fascinate me, Jocelyn Overstreet. You are unlike any woman I've ever known."

"I am not so very different from other women."

"You are wrong about that. You are special."

She gave her head a slight shake. "I will return to New York at the end of the summer."

"And I will return to England in the spring." He put his hands on her shoulders, wanting to draw her closer but resisting the urge. "And I want you to come with me, Jocelyn."

Her eyes widened, the gold flecks reflecting the evening sunlight falling through the window. "Come with you?"

"Yes. Come with me. To England. I am asking you to be my wife."

She sucked in a quick breath as she took a step away from him.

He wanted to reach for her, to pull her close again.

"Mr. Whitcombe, if I have done anything to make you think—"

"Sebastian. Call me Sebastian."

"I'm sorry," she whispered before hurrying from the room.

He felt her going like a blow. What had come over him? Why had he kissed her? Why had he announced his intentions? It was too soon. He'd rushed her. Perhaps he should have spoken with William first. But the way she'd looked at him. The way her lips had tasted upon his. He'd thought . . . He'd hoped . . . He'd wanted . . .

He sank onto the chair Jocelyn had sat on only a short while before and covered his face with his hands. *Father in heaven, did I move out ahead of You? Forgive me. Help me make things right.* He lowered his hands and saw Mrs. Adler standing in the doorway to the kitchen.

"What happened here?" Her gaze took in the untouched meal and the place where he sat. "Where is Miss Joss?"

He answered with a shake of his head.

The look she gave him made it clear that whatever progress he might have made toward making her like him had been erased in the blink of an eye.

JOCELYN SAT at her dressing table, staring at her reflection without seeing.

What have I done? What have I let him do?

Marry him. He wanted her to become his wife, to

leave her country and go with him to England. It was preposterous. Couldn't he see that? Utterly preposterous.

She touched her mouth. It was almost as if she could still feel his lips upon hers. So soft. So tender. Years ago, on the evening of his proposal, Robert Burnett had also kissed her. But that kiss had been nothing like Sebastian's. Robert's kiss had confirmed she wasn't in love with him. But Sebastian's kiss? Oh, Sebastian's kiss. It had made her feel—

"Miss Joss?" came Mrs. Adler's voice from the other side of the bedroom door. "May I come in?"

Jocelyn sniffed, only then realizing her vision had blurred with tears. She brushed at her eyes. "Yes."

The door opened. "What's wrong?" the housekeeper asked softly.

She twisted around on the stool. "He asked me to marry him."

Mrs. Adler sputtered in disbelief.

Jocelyn wiped away another tear. "I didn't . . . I didn't say no."

"Oh, Miss Joss." The older woman sat on the foot of the bed.

"I . . . I wanted to say yes, Mrs. Adler."

"Oh, Miss Joss."

She drew in a long, slow breath and released it. "I think . . . I think I may be falling in love with him."

Dear Adam,

Much has happened in the weeks since I last sat down to write to you.

Amanda returned from the visit to her friend with a new horse. A Palouse mare she hopes to breed with Glenhaven, if you and Eliza will allow it. The young mare is quite striking. I am convinced you will approve.

A week after her return from Washington, Amanda fell ill with a fever. She gave me quite a fright. William's sister and the housekeeper took excellent care of her, and she is now greatly improved, even though the doctor continues to impose rest. A rest she greatly resents.

Amanda's illness prevented us from going with Roger Bernhardt into Yellowstone National Park. It is a disappointment for us both, but I believe there will be other opportunities for us to do so. I am sure Roger will return from his adventures with many stories to tell as well as many paintings.

And now for the reason I sat down to write to you. As before, I wish I could walk to your cottage or down to the stables and ask for your advice. But a letter will have to suffice. Perhaps the simple act of writing to you will bring clarity.

In my last letter I told you I wished to marry Miss Overstreet, and I explained some of my concerns. I hope I also explained some of my reasons for wanting this marriage. My plan was to make her fond of me. To make her care for me a great deal. And only then to begin to plant thoughts of England in her mind. Appealing thoughts, I hoped.

But I spent today with her in William's office, reconciling some of the accounts of this large ranch. We talked some, but we were also silent for long periods. Yet I was aware of her every moment of those many hours. Then, after only a short break, we sat down to eat together. William has gone to the town of

Pocatello on a matter of business, and Amanda took a tray in her room. Roger, as I indicated above, is now painting and drawing his way through the park. Therefore, it was only the two of us once again, this time in the dining room.

Adam, something overcame me, and I kissed her. I could not even tell you how, precisely, it happened. Afterward I told her I wished to marry her, that I wanted her to return to England with me. She fled the room.

I fear I may have scared her away before I had the chance to truly win her affections, and now I must find a way to overcome whatever damage I have done. Were she to leave the ranch today and go back to New York, I believe I would follow her there.

There are many things I do not know, but this I am sure of. I want Jocelyn Overstreet as my bride and will settle for no other.

Your brother,
Sebastian Whitcombe

Chapter Sixteen

After a restless night, Jocelyn rose before the sun. She dressed with haste, then wove her hair into a single braid. Walking as silently as possible, she descended the stairs and made her way to the kitchen.

"Good morning, Mr. Kincaid."

Chuck looked up from the cutting board. "You're up plenty early, Miss Joss."

"I'm going for a ride while the morning's still cool. Is there something to eat I can take with me?"

"Got some dried apples. And there's fresh biscuits, if that'll do you."

"Yes, please."

He wrapped the promised items in a cloth. "Here you go." He handed the bundle, along with a canteen, to Jocelyn. "Best let one of the boys know what direction you're riding since you're goin' out alone."

"I will."

"You be careful now."

She gave him a quick smile as a promise to do as he

bid, then she exited through the back door off the kitchen. Cowboys moved about the barnyard in the weak early morning light, readying for the day. Chickens clucked in the coop off to the left side of the barn. One of the dogs ran up to give Jocelyn a sniff, then trotted alongside her as she went to the barn.

She saddled and bridled Bella while her mind replayed moments from the previous day. Moments when she'd looked up from the ledger and found Sebastian watching her, his expression tender and thoughtful. Moments when they'd laughed together. The moment when he'd kissed her.

Her breath caught at that memory, and she pressed her forehead against the saddle. "What am I to do?" she whispered.

The dog nudged the back of her knee with its nose.

"Sorry, boy. I have nothing for you." She straightened, gathered the reins, stepped into the saddle, and rode out of the barn. She spied the ranch foreman almost at once. "Jake."

He stopped and turned. "Morning, Miss Jocelyn. Didn't expect to see you out here this early."

"I spent yesterday shut up in William's office. I need to go for a ride to clear my head. Mr. Kincaid told me to make sure someone knew what direction I'm going."

"Always a good thing to do."

She glanced toward the east, then the west. A tug in her heart made her decision for her. "I'm going to ride into town. Tell Mrs. Adler not to worry if I'm not back until afternoon."

"I'll do it, miss." He tugged the brim of his hat.

Jocelyn pressed her heels into Bella's sides, and the mare walked out of the barnyard. A long shadow went before her as she continued west toward Gibeon, the rising sun at her back. Eventually, Jocelyn asked for more speed from her mount, a trot at first and then a slow canter. The mare's rolling gait drew the tension from Jocelyn, and for a short while, she forgot everything except for the beauty of the passing countryside—the gentle rise and fall of the land, the grasses that had turned from green to gold as the season passed, the stands of pines and aspens, the mountain ranges in the distance. Only the rhythm of Bella's hooves upon hard-packed earth broke the silence of the morning.

She would be happy in Idaho. She could make it her permanent home. She'd scarcely given thought to the shipping company in the past two months. If she and William decided to sell Overstreet Shipping, she would be able to stay on Eden's Gate for good. Selling would also solve the ranch's financial problems for the foreseeable future.

"Come with me. To England. I am asking you to be my wife."

Jocelyn eased back on the reins, slowing Bella to a walk.

Would she be happy if she went to England? She'd never crossed the ocean as William had, never traveled abroad. Her brother had enjoyed many aspects of his school years. Not all aspects, but many. He'd formed friendships, too. A lasting one with Sebastian. True, William was happier in Idaho on the ranch, but he hadn't hated England.

"I am asking you to be my wife."

It was possible she would like England . . . but would she be happy as Sebastian's wife? She hadn't yearned for marriage as some women did. She liked her independence. Some husbands made every decision. Some ruled with iron thumbs.

Would Sebastian be that kind of husband? What did she know about him, really?

His brown eyes were expressive.

His thick hair made her want to run her fingers through it, made her want to push it off his forehead.

She loved his accent.

In the evenings, a shadow of a beard always darkened his jaw. Would it feel prickly or soft to the touch?

He could be thoughtful.

He could tease.

His laughter was delicious.

He was generous with his time and with his concern.

He loved his sister, and he was loyal to his friends.

"Come with me. To England. I am asking you to be my wife."

She frowned. Sebastian hadn't mentioned *why* he wanted to marry her. He hadn't declared his inability to live without her. He hadn't said he loved her. Robert Burnett had claimed all of that, but it hadn't been true. Wasn't it better to know the truth?

She drew the mare to a halt. Closing her eyes, she whispered, "Father, if I am to marry, I want it to be for love." She took a slow breath and released it. "Is that foolish of me?"

Last night she'd told Mrs. Adler she might be falling in love with Sebastian. In the light of a new day, she knew there was no "might" about her feelings. She was already in love with Sebastian Whitcombe.

WHEN SEBASTIAN OPENED the door to his bedroom, he saw his sister standing at the top of the stairs, about to descend.

"Joining us for breakfast?" he asked as he walked toward her.

"Yes. I'm not staying in that bedchamber one more minute. I don't care what you or Mrs. Adler or the doctor say."

He grinned. "You definitely sound more like yourself."

"You have no idea, brother."

He lifted his hands in a sign of surrender. Then he motioned for her to proceed him down the stairs.

As Sebastian had dressed for the day, he'd played out several different scenarios in his mind about the moment he would see Jocelyn again. He'd imagined what she might say or do when they met at the breakfast table. He'd practiced what he might say to her in return. Of course, she might try to avoid him today. That wouldn't be good. Worse, she might decide to leave Eden's Gate and return to New York.

But then he'd remembered the kiss they'd shared. She hadn't pulled away. Her lips had lingered upon his. That gave him reason to hope.

As he followed his sister into the dining room, he

looked hopefully toward Jocelyn's chair. It was empty. In his memory, he heard her say, *"I'm sorry."*

Now he was the one who wanted to apologize. He was sorry for upsetting her. Sorry for moving too fast. Sorry for not explaining himself better. Sorry he might have ruined his chances with her.

The housekeeper entered the dining room carrying a serving bowl.

"Good morning, Mrs. Adler," Amanda said cheerfully.

"Good morning, Miss Whitcombe. You're looking more like yourself."

"I'm feeling well too. I didn't cough much at all in the night."

"Well, don't overdo your first day out of bed." The older woman turned toward the kitchen doorway.

"Mrs. Adler," Sebastian said.

She stopped and looked back at him.

"Has Jo— Has Miss Overstreet been down to breakfast yet?"

"She was down but not for breakfast. She went for a ride, I was told." Mrs. Adler gave him a hard look filled with blame. "There was something troubling her."

He glanced toward the window, then back at the housekeeper. "How long ago did she leave?"

"Can't say. I didn't see her myself. But I'm sure the sun was hardly up." She folded her hands beneath her ample bosom. With obvious reluctance, she added, "Ask Jake Foster, if he's still about. He might know." With that she turned and disappeared into the kitchen.

"Sebastian?" Amanda frowned. "What was that about?"

"I need to see Jocelyn. I need to talk to her."

"I'm sure she'll be back soon."

He rubbed a hand over his face, a sense of panic rising in his chest.

"Sebastian?" His sister's hand alighted on his shoulder. "Whatever is wrong?"

"I asked her to marry me last night."

Amanda sucked in a breath.

"I think . . . I'm afraid I made a mistake. My proposal upset her."

Amanda took his hand and tugged him toward a chair, motioning for him to sit. He did as she bid.

"Now." She turned the nearest chair to face him, then sat on it. "Tell me about this proposal of yours."

During the night, he'd gone over everything in his mind at least a hundred times. Now he relayed it to his sister, from the moment at breakfast when he'd offered to help Jocelyn in William's office all the way through to the moment Jocelyn had whispered her regret and fled the dining room.

Amanda frowned at him. "You kissed her."

"Yes."

"And she kissed you back."

"I would say so, yes."

"And then you told her you wanted her to go to England with you as your wife."

Frustrated, he answered again, "Yes."

"And did you think to mention how much you care for her?"

He drew back.

Amanda sighed. "Did it not occur to you that words of affection could make a difference?"

"Well, no. But—"

"It isn't as if family members have arranged a match for you both. Any woman would want to know *why* you wish to marry her. Jocelyn may need your reasons even more than others. After all, she doesn't *need* to marry. She is capable of running a successful company. She has brains as well as beauty. She has money of her own. She has a loving brother. Why would she give up all that to go with you to England as your wife?"

"Because . . ." He felt his eyes widen. "I don't know why she would give it up. I only know I cannot imagine going back to Hooke Manor without her at my side."

Amanda smiled. "Perhaps you *love* her?"

Love. Did he love Jocelyn? He'd been attracted to more than one woman in the past. This was more than mere attraction. But did that make it love?

"Sebastian." Amanda gave her head a slow shake. "You know more about your feelings than you think you do."

He stood. "You're right. And I need to talk to her." He strode from the dining room, determined to do exactly that as soon as possible.

Chapter Seventeen

ibeon remained quiet when Jocelyn rode her
horse up to the front of the church. After she
dismounted and tied Bella to the hitching post, she went
to the front door and opened it. "Reverend
Blankenship?"

Silence answered her.

She moved through the small vestibule into the sanctuary where she sat in the center of the back pew.

If I am to marry, I want it to be for love. She'd prayed
those words on the road into town. This time she added,
*I already love him. Is that enough? Is it necessary for him to love
me as well?*

She covered her face with her hands, leaning
forward at the waist.

Father, please answer me.

Sebastian was a viscount, a member of the British
peerage, and he would one day become an earl. What
would that make her? A lady of some kind, she
supposed. But did it matter? The real question was, did

she want the kind of life that would come with a title and a manor house and estates?

The upper echelons of New York society often behaved as if they were members of the aristocracy. A few she'd witnessed had behaved abominably toward others. Rude and thoughtless and entitled. Believing themselves superior to everyone around them because of their great wealth. But Sebastian and his sister weren't like that. Was that only because they were on a ranch in the American West, away from their family and peers? Would their behavior change once they returned to England and were with people of their own class?

A throat cleared behind her. She straightened and her hands fell away from her face. As she turned her head, the reverend stepped into view in the side aisle.

"Miss Overstreet." Surprise laced his voice. "I didn't expect to find anyone here this early on a Saturday."

"Good morning, Reverend Blankenship." She stood. "I'm not disturbing you, am I?"

"You are always welcome in God's house."

She sank onto the pew again as her gaze went toward the cross behind the pulpit. "I wanted to think. To pray. So I came here."

"Do you wish to be alone?"

She looked at him again. "No. I—" She shook her head. "I don't know."

The pastor took another step forward and sat at the end of the pew in front of her. "I'm a good listener."

Based upon his bowed head, Jocelyn suspected he added a silent prayer. Then he sat, still and silent. Waiting.

After a long while, Jocelyn asked, "How does God speak to you?"

He swiveled in the pew until their gazes met. "That wasn't what I expected you to ask me, Miss Overstreet."

She could have told him it wasn't what she'd expected to ask either, but now she realized she desperately wanted the answer. She'd asked God to speak to her. But what if He answered and she couldn't discern His voice?

Reverend Blankenship cleared his throat as he looked forward again. "First I would tell you God is not limited in His ability to speak to people in ways I may not understand. Still, here is what I am sure of. The Holy Spirit indwells those who follow Christ, and it is He who speaks to us."

Even though the reverend wasn't looking at her, Jocelyn nodded.

"I believe God most often speaks to His children through the Bible. It is the inspired Word of God, and it reveals His story of restoration for a fallen world. It is a guide for us, and it is quick and powerful and sharper than any two-edged sword. You would do well to read it earnestly. But God also speaks into a believer's heart, and the more we listen for Him and to Him, the more we will recognize His voice. God also speaks to us through His body of believers, and He speaks to us through our circumstances. All kinds of circumstances. The good and the bad." He paused for a moment, then added, "'And we know that all things work together for good to them that love God, to them who are the called according to his purpose.'"

She recognized the verse from the book of Romans and whispered, "Amen."

"Miss Overstreet." The reverend turned once again, this time holding onto the back of the pew with his right hand, his arm outstretched. "If you have asked God a question and diligently seek His answer, I promise He will speak to you. What I cannot promise is that the answer will come quickly. Sometimes we must wait and trust. Waiting can be difficult. But the answer will come." He fell silent, as if to prove his point about waiting. Finally, he asked, "Is that of any help to you?"

She offered a quick smile. "Yes, it does help." She heard Sebastian's voice from the previous night, saying he wanted her to be his wife. She heard her heart reminding her that she was in love with Sebastian. She released a humorless laugh as the memories faded. "But I would prefer a quick answer. I am not particularly good at waiting."

"Few of us are, Miss Overstreet. Few of us are."

SEBASTIAN HAD PUSHED Goldrush hard all the way to Gibeon. But when he spied Jocelyn's mare tied to the post outside of the church, he eased back on the reins, bringing the gelding to a walk. His pulse took longer to slow to a normal pace.

Now what should he do? It hadn't occurred to him he would find her in the church. Should he go in? Should he wait for her to come out? Should he turn around and ride back to the ranch? He reined in

Goldrush and looked behind him. While Sebastian had been in the dining room with Amanda, it seemed imperative he talk to Jocelyn as soon as possible. But now . . . now he questioned his impulsiveness. It appeared she'd needed time with God. Who was he to intrude? He looked forward again, undecided.

The door to the church opened, and Reverend Blankenship appeared on the stoop. He paused and rubbed his chin thoughtfully before his gaze went to Jocelyn's horse. A moment longer, and the pastor looked beyond Bella and found Sebastian seated on Goldrush. He lifted his hand in a half-wave. What could Sebastian do but nudge his horse forward, closing the distance between them?

Reverend Blankenship came down the steps.

"Good morning." Sebastian stopped Goldrush a second time.

"Morning."

Sebastian dismounted and tied his horse next to Jocelyn's. As he turned toward the pastor, he said, "I . . . uh . . . Is Miss Overstreet inside?"

"She is, indeed."

"Have you spoken with her?"

"I have."

"Is she . . . is she all right?"

If Reverend Blankenship was surprised by his questions, his expression gave no hint of it. "She is fine, but she's seeking answers from the Lord. I believe you should leave her in peace, Mr. Whitcombe." There was a firmness in the pastor's voice that brooked no argument, even from a man many years Sebastian's junior.

He gave a nod. "I shall do that."

Reverend Blankenship waved toward the main street. "Would you care to join me for coffee at Miss Irene's? She serves a good breakfast, too, if you haven't eaten. Nothing fancy but good and filling."

He hadn't eaten breakfast. He'd left Eden's Gate without even putting food on his plate, let alone eating it. He'd missed dinner the night before too. Suddenly he realized he was famished. Perhaps that was God's way of keeping him from rushing into the church and demanding an answer from Jocelyn—something more than the words, "I'm sorry."

"I will join you, reverend."

"Good. Very good."

As they walked into town, Reverend Blankenship asked, "How are you finding your visit to America?"

"Unexpected."

The reverend laughed. "In a good way?"

"Yes. At least, I hope so."

They arrived at the restaurant, and the reverend stepped forward to open the door, waving Sebastian through ahead of him. The interior of Miss Irene's smelled of bacon and coffee and woodsmoke. There were eight tables at the front of the building, each table with four chairs around it. Many of those chairs were occupied, and the clink of utensils on plates and the hum of conversations filled the air.

"Morning, reverend," a woman with a shock of red curls beneath a white cap called from the back of the room. "Take a seat. I'll bring your coffee right out."

Reverend Blankenship grinned. "I come here every

day of the week but Sunday. I can't seem to make coffee as good as Miss Irene's."

They sat opposite each other at a vacant table. Sebastian took a moment to look around the small restaurant. He'd attended church services in Gibeon the previous three Sundays, and he recognized some of the other diners. When he received a few nods, he returned them in kind.

The reverend said, "Gibeon's a friendly town."

"I have found it so."

"I came here three years ago. Felt at home almost from the first moment the stagecoach rolled into town."

"Three years?" He looked at the other man. "If you don't mind me saying so, you seem awfully young to have been pastoring a church that long."

"I'm twenty-four, and you would not be the first to question if I am old enough to shepherd a congregation. I received the call to preach when I was seventeen, and later God laid it on my heart to serve His children out west. I was a circuit preacher for a couple of years, but Gibeon is where my calling finally led me."

"I apologize if my words were insulting."

"They were not insulting, and you need not be sorry for them. In the beginning, even I wondered if my youth was a disadvantage. Then the good Lord used a passage in Jeremiah to calm my doubts and fears. It says, in part, 'Say not, I am a child: for thou shalt go to all that I shall send thee.'"

"I envy you, reverend. Such a strong and clear answer."

"It has sustained me through the years."

"I take it you are not married."

The younger man chuckled. "I have not been so blessed. Not yet." He fell silent when the waitress arrived with two cups of steaming black coffee. "Thank you, Miss Irene."

"Do you want anything else?" she asked, looking from the reverend to Sebastian.

Sebastian nodded. "Yes, please. I would like breakfast."

"Been a busy morning. You gotta get here early on a Saturday if you want your choice from the full menu. We're running short of some items. No steaks left. No bacon or fried taters either. Will sausages, biscuits, and eggs do you?"

"That would be fine."

"I'll have it out in a jiff." She slipped away between tables and chairs, disappearing through swinging doors into the kitchen.

When Sebastian looked at the reverend again, he saw the other man smile as he took his first sip of coffee. It was a look of pure bliss, one Sebastian didn't understand. He much preferred tea to coffee. Still, so as not to offend either the man across from him or Miss Irene herself, he lifted the cup to his lips.

"I am not married," the reverend said, as if there'd been no break in their conversation. "But am I correct to think you might want to be?"

Sebastian nearly choked on his coffee. As he set down his cup, he cleared his throat. Was he that transparent? "Reverend Blankenship—"

"Perhaps it would be easier for us to have a friendly

conversation if you called me by my Christian name." The reverend put out his hand across the table. "My name is Truman."

He shook the proffered hand. "Sebastian."

"Now tell me." Truman Blankenship smiled. "Am I correct about you and Miss Overstreet?"

"I see you do not easily let go of an idea."

"My mother always said I was like a bulldog."

Sebastian laughed even as he decided, if he couldn't talk to his brother Adam, he might as well talk to a man of the cloth.

Chapter Eighteen

As Jocelyn sat in the pew, praying and thinking, she replayed the moments and hours she'd spent with Sebastian since that first day back in May right up to last night when he'd asked her to marry him. The memories were all so clear to her, but they came not with answers but rather with more questions. It must have been an hour or more since Reverend Blankenship had left her alone in the sanctuary, but if God had spoken to her during that time, she hadn't heard Him.

With a sigh, she rose. "Oh Lord, tell me what to do," she whispered again. Then she moved to the aisle and walked out of the silent church.

Jocelyn paused after stepping through the doorway, and her breath caught. Goldrush was tied to the hitching rail near Bella. She swept her gaze across the churchyard, looking for Sebastian. She found him walking toward her down the main street. Reverend Blankenship was beside him. The two of them stopped, and the pastor said something to Sebastian. Then he turned in a different direction. Sebastian continued on alone, his eyes never straying from hers.

"I . . . I didn't expect to see you in town," she said when he came to a stop at the bottom of the steps.

"Jake told me you rode this way."

"I needed some time to think. Riding usually helps me see things from a clearer perspective."

"Did the ride help today?"

She gave a slight shake of her head. "Not entirely."

"Perhaps *I* can help." He removed his hat. "If you'll allow me."

She found herself wishing she'd already descended the steps. She found herself wishing she was back in his arms, his lips upon hers.

"Last night," he said. "Perhaps I moved too quickly last night. I am sorry."

Did he regret kissing her? Even more, did he regret asking her to return to England with him as his wife? She reached for the handrail to steady herself.

"Miss Overstreet . . . Jocelyn . . . I failed to express myself well. I would like to try to do better."

Try to do better? So he wasn't withdrawing his proposal?

He held out a hand, inviting her to come down the steps. She couldn't resist. She didn't want to resist. A few short steps, and her left hand was enveloped in his right one. But when she might have moved closer, he stopped her with a firm shake of his head.

"Let me say what I came here to say."

Her breath caught again, and she held very still.

"Jocelyn, for some years now my father has pressured me to marry and start a family. Out of duty to the Whitcombe name, I need to produce an heir for the earldom. I have resisted, not because I do not want a wife and children, but because I was not willing to marry someone for what I believe would be the wrong reasons. I wish to have shared interests and shared affections with my wife. I believe that is true of you and me, despite the short amount of time we have known each other. I believe love will come with time."

He does not love me. At least not yet. The truth stung her heart. *But he believes we share affection for each other.* That gave her hope. *He believes we will learn to love.* Was that enough for now?

"My parents' union was arranged," he continued. "They barely knew each other on their wedding day, but they were happy together and love grew between them. I was fortunate to witness that love for myself."

"I saw the same between my parents," she responded softly. "But they were very much in love from the start. Or so they always told us."

His grip tightened on her hand. "I will not pretend there will not be challenges. You would be a stranger to England, and undoubtedly a stranger to the ways of the British aristocracy. But I promise, if you agree to be my wife, I will protect you and guide you as you gain your footing. I would do whatever was in my power to see that you are happy in your new home."

It was the tenderness in his eyes that undid her, that made her forget to be cautious and to wait for a word from the Lord. "Yes."

He blinked. "Yes?"

"Yes, Sebastian. I will marry you."

His surprised expression slowly transformed into a smile. "By heavens, that is good news. I won't let you be sorry, Jocelyn."

As Sebastian expected, his sister received the news of the engagement with joy and enthusiasm. "I couldn't be happier," Amanda said as she embraced Jocelyn. "I always wanted a sister. Six months ago, I had none, and now I will have two, thanks to my brothers." She released Jocelyn and hugged Sebastian. "You have made a wonderful choice in a wife."

"That I have." He smiled, reveling in the moment.

His sister released him and turned to face Jocelyn. "When will William be back?"

"Before supper. Maybe even by this afternoon."

"Oh, I can't wait to see his face when he hears the news."

Sebastian could only hope his friend would be pleased. While he didn't need William's permission to marry Jocelyn, he did desire his blessing. If only he could hope for a blessing from the earl.

"You are thinking about Father," Amanda said.

"How did you know?"

"Your frown." His sister leaned toward him and lowered her voice. "Will you write to him at once?"

"I'll send a transatlantic cable on Monday. This isn't the kind of news I can put in a letter."

If only he could. A letter to the earl by regular post

had to cross the American interior by train, sail over the ocean, and travel by mail coach to the village near Hooke Manor. A journey that would take a minimum of two weeks. Two weeks before he had to worry about receiving an angry reply from his father via cable. Sending his own cable first meant he would have only a day or two to wait for an answer.

He looked at Jocelyn who was now talking to Mrs. Adler on the opposite side of the parlor. He hadn't told his intended anything about the earl. Especially not his father's disdain for Americans. Was that fair to her? The earl could be an intimidating, stern sort of man in the best of circumstances. When thwarted, he became unrelenting in his opposition.

Jocelyn turned her head, and their gazes met across the room. He felt his frown melt away, replaced by a smile. He had crossed an ocean to find this woman—although he hadn't known that was his destiny—and he would not let his father spoil what he'd found. No matter what the return cable might have to say, Jocelyn was in his life to stay.

———

AT SUPPER THAT EVENING, Jocelyn looked across the table at Sebastian and had the urge—not for the first time that day—to pinch herself to see if she were dreaming. Was this real? Was it truly happening? Had she agreed to marry him and move to England?

William had been both surprised and pleased when he'd heard the news of his sister's engagement to

Sebastian and had said so more than once during the evening meal. Amanda's contributions to the conversation had flitted from the topic of where and when the two of them should marry, to the English friends she couldn't wait for Jocelyn to meet, to wondering who among the peerage would throw the first ball for the new Viscountess Willowthorpe. It all made Jocelyn's head spin.

When supper ended, William excused himself, saying he had work to do in his office before he would be able to retire for the night. As soon as her brother strode from the dining room, Amanda stated she had a letter to write, and a moment later, she was gone as well.

Sebastian stood. "If I am not mistaken, William and Amanda want us to enjoy some time alone." He rounded the table and eased her chair back from the table. "Will you join me on the porch? It should be pleasant outside by now."

Was it possible to feel hot and cold at the same time?

She took his offered hand and allowed him to draw her up from the chair. Then, as if they'd been doing so for years, he tucked her hand into the crook of his arm and walked with her toward the front of the house. Outside, the heat of day lingered, and the air was still and silent. The sun, low in the western sky, splashed shades of gold across the granite peaks of the mountains in the east.

Sebastian escorted Jocelyn to the nearest chair, but before she could settle on it, he turned her to face him. His fingers cradled her chin, causing her to look up.

"Are you content with your decision, Jocelyn?"

Her throat went dry, and her breathing felt shallow. She nodded.

"You don't regret saying you will marry me?"

"No." She only regretted he hadn't kissed her all day long. Shouldn't an engagement be sealed with a kiss?

A smile tugged at the corners of his mouth. "We haven't had a moment's peace since we got back from Gibeon."

Had he read her thoughts and offered an explanation for why he hadn't kissed her? That's how it seemed to her in the moment before his head lowered and his lips met hers.

When they'd kissed the previous evening, it had been like the brush of a butterfly's wings. So light. So tender. Too brief. This time was different. Sebastian held her close, and his lips seemed to demand more from her. She lifted her arms to circle his neck and gave in to the sensations.

Learn to love me, Sebastian. That's all I ask. Love me.

He broke the kiss after a long while, pulling back but leaving his mouth tantalizingly near. She relished the feel of his warm breath on her skin. She was not skilled in the art of love, but she was certain his pulse raced as fast as her own, and a thrill of delight shivered up her spine.

He cleared his throat as he took a small step backward. "We should talk."

She didn't want to talk. She wanted to return to his embrace and kiss him again. But she sank onto the chair, only then realizing how weak her legs had become.

He sat nearby, his expression serious. "My sister

reminded me at supper that there are many details we should discuss. Normally, at least in England, there would be a marriage contract negotiated. The dowry would be discussed. Property would be considered." He took her hand. "If you were an American heiress in search of a title and I were a British peer in search of a rich dowry to support my estates, a contract would matter a great deal. But we are not those two people. We are not interested in money or prestige. We are a man and woman, free and independent and able to choose for ourselves. We wish to build a life together because we like each other."

Was it possible her pulse raced faster now than when he'd kissed her?

"Am I right, Jocelyn?" There was a note of uncertainty in his question.

"Yes."

"Good. Then let us speak of the wedding. Where do you wish it to take place?"

Without hesitation, she answered, "Here. In the church in Gibeon."

"Here?" Surprise filled his brown eyes.

It was her turn to feel uncertain. "Is that wrong? Don't you like that idea?"

"No. It isn't that. Only I thought you might like a . . . larger affair."

"I would rather have people I know and consider friends. But of course, I'm not thinking of you. Of the friends *you* might wish to be present. Do you want a larger affair?"

He grinned. "No, I do not. I rather like the idea of

marrying without much fanfare. Just friends and family as witnesses. Amanda and Roger are already here, and except for Adam and Eliza, there is no one else I would desire to have present. We would then return to England as man and wife. A *fait accompli*." He gently squeezed her hand, then released it and settled back in his chair.

Jocelyn took a breath and did the same, turning her gaze upon the mountains. She wondered if she would ever see the Tetons again after she went to England with Sebastian. But at least she would have until next May before she would have to say goodbye to them.

Dear Adam,

I will send a cable to Father within a couple of days, so by the time this letter arrives by regular post, you will have long known my main reason for writing. But there is more I want to say to you, words I will not write in my cable to Father.

Miss Overstreet accepted my proposal. Amanda and William are both supportive of the marriage which is good. We shall not wait to marry in England. We plan to marry in Idaho in three weeks. A small affair with only friends and families present. I would have you and Eliza here with me, but I know that would complicate your relationship with Father, perhaps even threaten your employment on the estate.

A part of me believes we should call short our stay in America and return to England immediately after the wedding. Another part of me believes it would be best for us to remain until May, as previously planned. I am certain there will be a great deal of gossip about my American bride, no matter when we arrive.

Father will not be pleased with the idea of an American daughter-in-law, of course, and he will share his displeasure with others. Lest you think I chose Jocelyn in order to defy Father, I must say that is far from the truth. She will bring new life to Hooke Manor. When you meet her, you will understand. Even Father will like her if she is given a chance.

Your brother,
Sebastian Whitcombe

Chapter Nineteen

O n Wednesday afternoon, Sebastian watched his
bride-to-be exercise a two-year-old filly at the
end of a lunge line. Jocelyn was covered in the dust
rising from the dry earth as the horse loped in circles
around her, but Sebastian thought she looked beautiful
in her split skirt and wide-brimmed hat, her long hair in
its usual braid.

Much had been accomplished in the four days since
Jocelyn accepted his proposal. They'd not only decided
where they would marry—Gibeon—but when. They
would wed in early August, while summer still lingered
in this high country. The future of the shipping
company was still being discussed between Jocelyn and
her brother, but from what Sebastian could tell, it wasn't
a matter that distressed either of them. The only bone
of contention the past few days had been with his sister.
When Sebastian had suggested they might want to cut
short their stay in America, Amanda had dug in her
heels.

"I am not a child, Sebastian," she'd told him. "I am twenty-two, and I do not need a chaperone. Roger won't go back early either. You know he won't. The rent is paid, and William has made us welcome whether or not you and Jocelyn leave before spring."

The memory of their disagreement made him frown, and he wondered when he would get a reply to his cable. In fact, it surprised him that he hadn't received one already. His father was usually swift to share his disapproval.

"Amanda tells me I should take this filly with me to England."

Startled from his grimmer thoughts, he looked up to find Jocelyn and the young horse standing on the opposite side of the corral fence. Perspiration glistened on her forehead, and dirt smudged one of her cheeks. He thought her adorable and would have kissed her if not for the fence in his way.

Instead, he said, "My sister had best be content with taking her Palouse horse to England."

"I'll miss Bella. I'd forgotten what it's like to ride her across this range."

"We have many fine horses in the Hooke Manor stables. You'll find another favorite, I assure you."

The rattle of harness and clop of horses' hooves drew Sebastian around in time to see a coach roll into the barnyard. As it came to a creaking halt, Jake Foster left one of the outbuildings and walked toward the vehicle.

"Was William expecting company?" Sebastian asked Jocelyn.

"Not that I know of."

He faced her again. "Let's plan on a ride tomorrow morning when it's cooler. Just you and me."

She smiled and nodded, and at that moment, he would have let her take a hundred horses back to England with her if she wanted them.

"Blast you, man! Get that door open and let me out."

Everything in Sebastian turned cold at the familiar voice shouting orders. Slowly, he turned once again, in time to see his father descend from the coach. He appeared travel weary as well as somewhat thinner than three months earlier when Sebastian had ridden away from Hooke Manor. But the scowl on the earl's face remained very much the same as the last time they'd been together.

"Is this it? Is this Eden's Gate?"

"Yes, sir," Jake replied. "It is."

"And who are you?"

Before the foreman could answer, Amanda came out of the house. "Father!" She ran across the yard and embraced him in a tight hug. "Oh, it is good to see you. I cannot believe you're here. Why didn't you let us know you were coming?"

Edward Whitcombe would only allow one person in the world to hug him that way. His daughter. But even Amanda was not allowed to prolong such an elaborate show of affection. "There, there, my girl. That's quite enough." He set Amanda back from him. "Where is he?"

Sebastian watched as his sister glanced toward the

house, hesitated, then turned her gaze toward the corral. If he wasn't mistaken, even from such a distance, he saw an apology in the look she gave him.

Wait. What was their father doing here? Sebastian had only sent the cable two days ago. His father would have had to depart Hooke Manor a minimum of two weeks ago to be arriving now. Three weeks, more likely. And if that were the case, he couldn't possibly yet know about the engagement.

Dread knotted his gut. His father hadn't received his cable. He didn't know about Sebastian's plans to marry Jocelyn. Had something happened to Adam? If so, he'd said nothing to Amanda during their embrace or her demeanor wouldn't still be cheerful.

His father turned in his direction, then strode across the barnyard toward the corral. "Sebastian."

"Father. This is unexpected."

"No doubt." His gaze moved over Sebastian's shoulder.

"Is everything all right at Hooke Manor?"

"Except for your absence? Of course."

Sebastian wished he could enter the corral and put his arm around his fiancée, but he saw no way to delay what had to be done. "Father, may I introduce William's sister, Miss Jocelyn Overstreet." He glanced toward her. "Jocelyn, this is my father, Edward Whitcombe, Earl of Hooke."

"I apologize for my appearance, my lord. It is a pleasure to meet you."

Sebastian held back a smile of appreciation. Not once in the two months he'd known her had she used his title or called him "my lord." But it seemed she understood, even though Sebastian had said so little about his father, that the proper form of address would be important to the earl.

"Miss Overstreet." His father's gaze swung back to Sebastian. "I would like a word with you, my boy. But first I need to wash and have something to drink. The heat and dust have made my throat ache, and the journey to this . . . *place* . . . was not a pleasant one."

Amanda hurried over and hooked arms with the earl. "I'll take you inside, Father. Mrs. Adler, the housekeeper, will see you are settled and have everything you need." She gave Sebastian a pointed look. Then she gently guided their father toward the house, saying, "How long do you intend to stay?"

Yes, how long do you intend to stay? And what brought you here?

"Does he know?" Jocelyn asked.

He faced her again. "About the engagement?"

She nodded.

"He couldn't know. He would have been more than halfway across the country by the time I sent the cable. But it seems he has something to discuss with me, and it must be important to bring him to America, let alone to Idaho. I'll tell him of our plans to marry as soon as he is ready to talk."

Uncertainty flickered in her eyes.

"Don't worry. As I have been, he will be enchanted once he gets to know you."

Please, God. He turned toward the house. *Let that be true.*

Tears welled in Jocelyn's eyes as she settled on the foot of her bed, Sebastian's introduction echoing in her memory. *"Father, may I introduce William's sister . . ."* The words stung now, just as they had a short while before. She understood, of course. His father didn't know the two of them were engaged. He hadn't received the cable. Sebastian couldn't spring a fiancée on the man only minutes after his arrival. And yet it hurt to be introduced as William's sister and not something more. Something more, like a bride-to-be.

A rap on the door intruded on her pondering.

"Enter."

The door opened, and Amanda looked in. "I never dreamed Father would set foot in America."

Nerves whirled in Jocelyn's belly.

The younger woman entered the bedroom, closing the door behind her. "Don't worry, Jocelyn. He isn't nearly as imperious as he tries to appear."

Jocelyn had spent many, many days of the past decade seated at board tables, faced with men who thought themselves superior based solely on their gender. She'd known how to deal with those men. Why did she feel suddenly cowed and overwhelmed by Sebastian's father simply because he was an English lord? Well, that would not do. It would not do at all.

"I'll help you and Sebastian however I can," Amanda added before opening the door again. "Join us as soon as you can." Then she slipped out of the room.

Jocelyn took a few deep breaths to fortify herself.

Her emotions over the past few days had been all over the place. Happy. Scared. Peaceful. Intimidated. Frightened. Confident.

She didn't doubt she wanted to marry Sebastian, but she often doubted she would be an asset to him as a wife. But then he would kiss her and any doubts would scurry away . . . for a time.

But now his father had arrived at the ranch. Why? What did it mean?

Heaven, help her.

———

STANDING IN THE PARLOR, Sebastian saw the door to Jocelyn's bedroom open and his sister step onto the landing. Amanda smiled down at him before moving to the top of the staircase.

"Jocelyn needs a while to freshen up before she joins us," she said as she descended the steps, "and Father said he would be down soon."

"Did he indicate to you what brought him here?" He paced to the opposite end of the room, then back again. "He scoffed at our desire to see America. What would make him take this trip? He's never enjoyed traveling. Not even short distances. And he came alone. Without his valet. When was the last time he went anywhere without Hughes?"

"I do find that part quite strange, but I didn't ask. You know Father."

"It's more than strange."

"Perhaps he missed us."

Sebastian grunted. Of all possible reasons, that was the least likely.

A sound drew their gazes as their father appeared from the end of the upstairs hallway. Sebastian knew in his gut something wasn't right. This visit was more than peculiar. Something dire must have happened to put the earl on a ship to America.

He took a step forward as his father joined them in the parlor. "Is there anything you need, sir?"

"Only for us to find a place to talk privately."

Sebastian's misgivings increased. "We can use William's office. He's out on the north range today." He glanced at his sister.

She gave him a slight nod in return and slipped out of the room.

A short while later, Sebastian and his father were seated in the office. He couldn't help remembering the day he'd spent in here with Jocelyn, the way they had worked together, the camaraderie they'd shared. That day had led to his offer of marriage. Less than a week ago, but suddenly it felt further removed in time. He shifted uneasily in his chair.

"You are wondering what brought me to America," his father said.

"Yes. I trust everything is all right back home?"

The earl's gaze moved about the dark-walled room, no doubt thinking how small it was in comparison to the rooms he used at Hooke Manor.

Sebastian cleared his throat. "Amanda and I also wondered why you didn't bring Hughes with you."

"I did bring him. The man fell and broke his leg as

we were disembarking in New York. Terrible thing. I had to leave him behind while I continued on."

Sebastian's sense of foreboding deepened once again. The earl might not be the warmest of men, but he wasn't neglectful of the people who worked for him on his estates. For him to leave Matthew Hughes behind in a strange city seemed out of character.

"He wanted to come with me, of course, but it would have been hard for him to endure the remainder of the journey. That wouldn't do. Besides, although you and he may not believe it, I have been known to dress myself without the aid of a valet."

Sebastian relaxed a little.

"However, my reason for coming to America is serious, and it couldn't wait for your return in the spring."

The tension returned. "What is it, Father?"

"I have a cancer."

Sebastian's heart skipped a beat. His father had cancer. How was that possible? He was the sort of man who simply didn't allow himself to be ill.

"A tumor in my stomach. They tried to cut it out, but without much success."

"When did the surgery happen? Shouldn't you be back in England, getting treatment?"

"The surgery was performed at the end of April. I am done with hospitals. There isn't more the quacks can do for me other than try to control my pain." He patted his stomach. "I've lost a bit of weight. I shall lose more. I must be careful with my diet and take the medications they give me. Otherwise, I intend to live my life as normal." He leaned forward. "What is most important to me now is to see you married and prepared to take my place as the Earl of Hooke when the time comes."

"You're dying?" The words seemed to tear at his throat.

"We are all dying. Some of us simply sooner than others."

"How long?"

"Weeks. Maybe months. Perhaps even a year if I'm fortunate."

Sebastian rose from the chair and went to the lone window in the room. He stared out at the rolling grasslands beyond the nearby copse of trees. Only hours ago, he'd been happy. He'd foreseen a beautiful future with Jocelyn by his side. Now his father was dying. His father, who had always seemed invincible, indestructible, a force of nature. Sebastian couldn't imagine a world without Edward Whitcombe in it. And what of Amanda? His sister would be crushed by this news.

"Your life is about to change, Sebastian. Far more than you expect. At least that was true of me when I became the earl."

"I am grieved by this news, Father. What can I do for you?"

"There is only one thing I want now. For you to marry and continue the Whitcombe legacy."

He turned from the window. "I am going to be married, Father."

"I do not mean next year. I do not mean eventually. It needs to be soon. You need to return to England."

"I don't mean next year either. I have asked Miss Overstreet to marry me. A cable was sent to you at

Hooke Manor two days ago. But you weren't there to receive it."

"Miss Overstreet?" The earl drew back in his chair. "The young woman I met outside?"

"Yes."

"That . . . that *cowgirl* with the dirty face? You cannot be serious."

He bristled and fought to keep his voice level. "I am quite serious. And I will thank you not to speak of my intended that way."

"Son, you must think of your position."

"I am thinking of it. I made you a promise that I would marry, and I am keeping that promise with a woman who will bring me happiness."

"What makes her suitable to be the next Countess of Hooke?"

Sebastian drew in a long, slow breath and let it out. "Father, I believe we have said enough for now. I will not listen to you speak against Jocelyn, no matter the degree of your illness." He moved toward the door. "Amanda must be told why you've come. When you speak to her, please remember how much she loves you. This will be a terrible blow."

His father twisted on the chair. "I will take care, Sebastian. Please send her in to me."

Chapter Twenty

Jocelyn had been content in the past two months to dress for comfort and practicality. She'd lived in split skirts, loose-fitting blouses, and riding boots. Now she found herself wishing she'd brought more elegant attire with her from New York. But what she found in her wardrobe would have to do.

Her damp hair drying fast in the warmth of her bedroom, Jocelyn drew a dress from the wardrobe, a summer gown of canary yellow. The skirt was gracefully draped, and the corsage was belted with a deep-gold ribbon. In the city, she would have worn a straw hat to complete the daytime ensemble, but today she would leave her head unadorned.

She dressed with care, then finished arranging her hair. Finally, she checked herself in the mirror one last time. Her appearance might not be suitable for an English ballroom, but it was definitely better than when she'd stood beside the filly in the corral. Was it enough to redeem herself with her future father-in-law? She could only hope.

When she opened her bedroom door, she heard nothing but silence. A silence that left her uneasy as she stepped onto the landing. Was she alone in the house? She had her answer as she went down the stairs. The three members of the Whitcombe family were seated in the parlor. Sebastian's expression was grim. Amanda looked as if she'd been crying. The earl's eyes, when he turned to look in Jocelyn's direction, were filled with what appeared to be resentment.

Sebastian stood and came to her. "You look lovely," he said softly.

"What is wrong?"

He gave his head a slight shake. "Let's go outside for a moment."

"You may tell her in front of me," the earl said.

Jocelyn looked from Sebastian to his father and back again.

After a few moments, Sebastian said, "My father traveled to Idaho to inform us that he is . . . ill."

"More than ill," the earl interrupted again. "I am dying."

She drew in a soft gasp, her fingers covering her mouth.

"And there are matters I must settle with my son that could not wait until this foolish trip of his ended next spring. It is doubtful I have that long."

Sympathy overcame Jocelyn's uncertainty. "I am very sorry about your health, Lord Whitcombe."

"The correct form of address is Lord Hooke."

"I . . . I'm sorry." She felt like a schoolgirl who'd been chastened by her teacher. "Lord Hooke."

Sebastian's hand alighted on her shoulder. "You weren't to know."

But she would have to know, wouldn't she? She had agreed to become a part of his world, a part of a society completely foreign to her. How often would she embarrass Sebastian before she learned everything her new position required?

"Young woman." The earl's tone was, if possible, more condescending than before. "You may as well know that I do not approve of my son's plans to take you for his wife."

"Father!"

"Sebastian will soon inherit the earldom. He will have great responsibilities, and he will need a woman of his own class by his side to help him perform his duties well. You are not of his class, Miss Overstreet. You are not even English. You do not know our way of doing things, our way of living."

Habit as much as confidence stiffened Jocelyn's spine. "You are absolutely correct, Lord Hooke. I am not of Sebastian's class nor am I English. I am an American, the daughter of two strong, determined people who made their way in a country that can be wild and harsh. They did it with resolution and the sweat of their brows, and they taught their children to work hard as well. I do not feel the need to apologize for who I am or for the family who made me what I am."

William's voice came from the dining room doorway. "Bravo."

She looked in her brother's direction, inordinately glad to see him. William was covered in dust, from his head down to his boots, much as Jocelyn had been upon the earl's arrival. William's face, tanned from all the hours he spent outdoors, looked even darker beneath the shadow of his wide-brimmed hat. He appeared to be exactly what he was. A rancher. A man who worked with his hands and who knew cattle and horses and who was willing to face down rattlesnakes, wolves, grizzly bears, the occasional bison, and even outlaws. Pride welled in her chest.

William moved into the parlor, his gaze sweeping from one person to the next. "What have I missed?"

Sebastian answered as he motioned toward the earl. "You remember my father."

"It's been a long time, Lord Hooke." William nodded but made no move to offer a hand.

"Indeed. You were just a lad when you visited our London house." The older man cleared his throat. "You've changed."

"I would hope so, sir. It's been a good fourteen years at least since we met." He put his arm around Jocelyn's shoulders and gave her a gentle squeeze, oblivious to the transfer of dust to her yellow dress. "And, as you said, I was still a boy at the time."

She wondered if he'd heard the earl call her unsuitable to be Sebastian's wife. Or had he caught only her response?

"I take it you've heard the good news, sir," William said. "About the engagement. Sebastian is a fortunate man, to be marrying my sister. Our housekeeper is in a frenzy, thinking of all that must be done to be ready for the wedding in August."

"August?" The earl was on his feet. "Sebastian, come to your senses."

"There is nothing wrong with my senses, Father. And as sorry as I am about your poor health, do not think that anything you say will change our plans."

Was that a flash of physical pain Jocelyn saw in the earl's eyes or was it a look of defeat?

The older man sat again. "I promise you, I will not say more about it for the rest of the day." He turned to Amanda. "Tell me about your adventures thus far, my dear. The last letter I received from you was all about a horse."

Despite her relief at the change of subject, Jocelyn felt sure this would not be the last time Lord Hooke shared his opinion about her unsuitability as a wife for his son.

Sebastian stepped closer to Jocelyn and whispered, "I need some air."

She glanced from him to William and back again, then slipped from beneath her brother's arm and walked with Sebastian to the front door. Neither of them said anything as they walked around the house to stand beneath the shade trees on the northeast corner.

Part of him wished he could smash his knuckles into something. Another part of him wanted to draw his intended into a comforting embrace. He did neither. "I'm sorry."

"It isn't your fault, Sebastian."

"I should have prepared you for how my father can be. I never expected him to show up here, but I still should have warned you."

"He says he's dying. What's wrong with him?"

"Cancer of the stomach."

"That's terrible. I'm so sorry, Sebastian."

He answered with a nod, then turned and stared into the distance.

His father was dying. Perhaps soon. Sebastian had thought he would have many years before he became the Earl of Hooke. He'd thought he had time to close the distance between him and his father. He'd thought he would have years to enjoy being married to Jocelyn, years to help her learn the way things were done in his world, years for her to come to know more of his friends, perhaps years for them to begin raising a family. He'd thought he had time, but it seemed time was running out. For all of them.

"Sebastian?"

"My father's illness doesn't change anything between us, Jocelyn."

"Perhaps it should. He came all this way. He must have many concerns. He must—"

He turned and pulled her to him, silencing her with his lips. He didn't want her to waver. He couldn't bear it if she changed her mind. She was the right woman for him, no matter what his father might think or say. If he could convince her in no other way that he was right, he would convince her with his kisses.

When he drew back from her at last, Jocelyn stared at him with sad eyes. "Tell me about your father."

"He is a complicated man, and we have always had a complicated relationship."

She gave him a fleeting smile.

"I have fallen short of his expectations for most of my life." He drew a breath and released it. "Since I was a boy, he's attempted to bully me into believing his way is the only way. He mostly failed in that regard. I have long been a disappointment as a son."

"I don't believe that. Surely he wouldn't come all this way if he didn't love you."

He considered her comment. "Perhaps he does. And I suppose I love him. But we aren't the sort of family who talks openly about our emotions. Father cared for Mother deeply, as I told you before. There was no disguising the way he felt about her or the way he grieved for her after she was gone. But it's much more difficult for him to show affection for his sons. His main concern at the moment is for the earldom and for the estates attached to the title. That's what compelled him to come all this way. He's afraid I will fail. Fail to provide an heir so the title stays with the Whitcombes and doesn't fall to a distant relative. Fail to protect the family's honor. That I will fail as the earl in all possible ways."

"Are *you* afraid you will fail?"

The question made him smile. Jocelyn knew how to get to the point. "No. I am not afraid of failing. In some respects, I know what is needed even more than my father does. I have been more involved in the day-to-day operations of Hooke Manor than he is or ever was." He cupped the side of her face with the palm of his hand. "And since I am to marry soon, I pray I will not fail to provide an heir while my father yet lives."

She lowered her gaze as a blush rose in her cheeks.

I hope we have many children together, Jocelyn. God willing.

Jocelyn closed her eyes. *Please, God. Let him learn to love me. And let it happen soon.*

Over the past few days, she had considered many things that would change once she married Sebastian. Her home would change. Her clothing would change. The people around her would change. But far more than that would change. She would soon share her life with this man. Her life . . . and her bed. She hadn't allowed her thoughts to go in that direction until he'd mentioned providing an heir.

The heat in her cheeks intensified.

She didn't know all the details of the act of marriage, but at her age, she wasn't completely ignorant. After all, she'd spent much of her life around cattle and horses, and she had heard the whispers of other women, even when they attempted to keep their unmarried friend in ignorance. No, she had some understanding . . . and she felt herself longing for the moment she would understand it all.

She looked up at Sebastian to find him watching her

with a tender gaze. Did he guess the direction of her thoughts?

"Stand firm with me, Jocelyn. Don't waver. You and I together, we will not fail."

Oh, how she hoped he spoke the truth.

Chapter Twenty-One

Sebastian stared at the ceiling, watching fingers of daylight inch across it. Most mornings he rose early, but he was tempted to remain here in bed until the heat of July drove him from the second-story bedchamber. Anything to avoid another confrontation with his father.

The previous evening had been difficult for everybody. Silence had ruled over the supper table, everyone conscious of the earl's disapproval. Disapproval of his son, of the engagement, of the ranch, of the country. When his father finally announced he would make an early night of it and retired to his room, the remaining diners had breathed a collective sigh of relief. And it hadn't been long before they'd all gone off to bed themselves.

What now? It was a question that had plagued Sebastian throughout the night. Would his father continue to badger him? Or would the earl change his methods? Would he turn on Jocelyn, try to undermine her in some way, try to break her will? The Earl of Hooke was accustomed to getting his own way. He was used to giving an order and having it obeyed immediately. But that wasn't happening now. His son was defying him, and his body was betraying him.

How long does he have, Lord? Can there be peace between us before it is too late?

Sebastian blew out a breath as he sat up and swung his legs over the side of the mattress. Avoiding his father wouldn't accomplish anything. Their problems wouldn't go away by ignoring them.

He took the time for a close shave, then dressed in the type of clothes all the cowboys on the ranch wore. As with everything else, his father wouldn't approve of his appearance, but he would have to get used to it for as long as he stayed at Eden's Gate.

And how long would that be? Would his father give up soon and go back to England? Or would he stay and continue to attempt to wreck his son's plans? Sunday, the fourth of August, hadn't seemed all that far off when he and Jocelyn set the date for the wedding. But seventeen more days suddenly seemed too long to wait. Too many things could go awry with his father staying here in the Overstreet home.

Sebastian released a groan. He might as well go downstairs and see what awaited him. As he stepped out of his room, he saw the door to the bedroom at the end of the hall swing open. His stomach sank a bit, but he mustered his resolve. "Good morning, Father."

The earl made a sound in his throat that might have been a greeting or might have been a complaint.

"I hope you slept well," Sebastian added as he moved forward.

"Well enough."

"I thought, if you felt up to it, I could show you around Eden's Gate this morning. There are some fabulous views of the grazing lands as well as the mountain ranges. We could take a buggy if you don't feel like riding."

"I am still able to sit a horse, thank you."

"Good. Then we'll plan on a tour of the ranch. After breakfast, before the day gets too hot."

The earl started down the stairs. Sebastian had noticed some weight loss upon his father's arrival yesterday. Now, as he followed behind him, he noticed more than that. His father's shoulders were rounded, his posture less than fully erect, and he moved with care, his hand holding tight to the bannister. It hit Sebastian afresh what the cancer was doing to his father, and his heart ached. He wished he could change the circumstances. Not just to drive out the cancer but to change their relationship. If only . . .

Mrs. Adler was setting the table when Sebastian and his father entered the dining room moments later. If any person alive could match the earl's look of disapproval, it was the Eden's Gate housekeeper. While Mrs. Adler had warmed to Sebastian over time, she had taken a quick dislike to the earl after learning he didn't think Jocelyn good enough to marry his son. Sebastian couldn't agree with Mrs. Adler more.

As if reading his mind, she turned a smile on Sebastian. "Good morning, sir." Then, without a glance in the earl's direction, she spun about and disappeared into the kitchen.

"Bless her," Sebastian said under his breath as he moved to his usual place.

His father huffed as he pulled out a chair. Undoubtedly he missed the footman who did that for him at Hooke Manor.

Sebastian searched his mind for something to say but came up blank. Much to his relief, his sister entered the room. He would trust her to guide the conversation.

"Good morning, Father." Amanda stopped behind the earl's chair, put her hands on his shoulders, and kissed the crown of his head.

"Amanda," he said, sounding gruff.

"I hope you slept well."

"Well enough, as I told your brother. The bed is good. Far better than the one in that wretched hotel in Pocatello. Miserable night there. But there were few options."

"It was the same for us." Amanda looked toward the empty sideboard before taking her seat.

"Amanda," Sebastian said, "I plan to show Father some of the ranch today."

"Oh, wonderful. I want to come. But before we do anything else, we must show him Ebony."

The earl raised a brow. "Ebony?"

"My new Palouse mare. Didn't you read my letter? I wrote to you about her. She is beautiful and incredibly swift. Adam is going to be thrilled when he sees her."

God bless his sister. Anything to do with horses was the least likely to prove controversial.

Before their father could respond, William and Jocelyn entered the dining room together. Sebastian stood and went to pull out the chair for Jocelyn. "How are you?" he asked softly.

She met his gaze. Her responding smile seemed sad to him. Mercy, he needed to change that.

"Sebastian and I are going to show Father around the ranch today," Amanda said. "You'll join us, won't you, Jocelyn?"

Sebastian noticed the way Jocelyn straightened her shoulders and seemed to gird herself for the day ahead.

"Of course." Jocelyn glanced in her brother's direction. "Billy, can you spare the time to come too?"

William nodded. "I can. It'll be good for Lord Hooke to get a view of an American cattle ranch." There was an edge to his voice that said, like the Eden's Gate housekeeper, he hadn't forgiven the earl for his rudeness.

It didn't look like this day would be any better than the one before.

MANY TIMES AT OVERSTREET SHIPPING, Jocelyn had stood toe-to-toe with disagreeable men. Powerful men. Determined men. Some men thought her incapable only because she was a woman, and she'd had to prove otherwise. She'd done so time and again. But never had she needed the strength to do so more than she did now.

Edward Whitcombe had been nothing but honest when he'd said he didn't approve of Jocelyn to be his son's wife. She couldn't blame him for feeling that way. She had doubts about her own suitability. But Sebastian had captured her heart. Utterly and completely captured it. She couldn't break the engagement because she couldn't bear the idea of not being with him. There was only one option open to her. Since she couldn't change her own mind about marrying Sebastian, she would have to change the earl's mind about her. She would have to earn his approval.

Her first opportunity came after breakfast.

Sebastian and William brought five horses out of the corrals and tied them to the hitching post in the shade of the barn. Soon William, Sebastian, Amanda, and Jocelyn set to brushing and currying them. The earl hung back, watching them with a frown.

"What's wrong?" Jocelyn asked in a hushed voice. "Doesn't he want to go after all?"

"He wants to go, but he's used to a groom getting his mount ready."

She moved away from Bella. "I'll do it."

Sebastian grinned, perhaps guessing her reason for offering.

Her brother had chosen a tall, well-muscled roan for the earl. While Red wasn't the handsomest horse on the ranch, the gelding had an easy gait, making him a pleasure to ride. She suspected William had chosen the horse for that reason.

Bless you, Billy.

After Red was saddled and bridled, she led him to the earl. "This is Red, Lord Hooke." She held out the end of the reins to the older man. "You'll find him an excellent ride."

The earl took the reins, although he didn't seem pleased to do so.

A short while later, everyone was mounted and ready to leave the barnyard. The earl's horrified expression when he saw the two women were both riding astride did not go unnoticed by any of them.

Amanda, seated on Ebony, said, "It is a safer way to ride, Father. I am ever so grateful to Jocelyn for encouraging me to give it a try."

Jocelyn winced. Amanda's praise would not earn her any favor with Edward Whitcombe.

"Sidesaddle is much more graceful and ladylike," the earl said. "Be assured, you will not ride like a hooligan once you are home at Hooke Manor."

"Father, what a thing to say." Amanda gave her head a toss as she pressed her heels into Ebony's sides. The mare trotted into the lead.

Jocelyn decided she would rather ride beside her future sister-in-law, even if it meant receiving visual daggers in the back from the earl. She encouraged Bella to catch up with the spotted mare.

Amanda glanced over. "Try not to let Father discourage you. He isn't always like this."

Isn't he? Jocelyn resisted the urge to look behind her.

"He has a gruff exterior but it's only skin deep. He isn't mean or cruel. Truly he isn't. But he can be quite blunt at times. He is more careful with his words with me. Much sharper with Sebastian. Adam too, but that is a different relationship."

Adam Faulkner. The illegitimate son of the earl. And despite the circumstances of his birth, he had married a lady to the manor born and apparently enjoyed some acceptance by friends of Sebastian and within the family.

Would Jocelyn ever be accepted into those same circles? Would she ever feel at home? She narrowed her eyes. A headache had begun to pound behind her temples. Perhaps she could outrun it. "Amanda, shall we race to the ridge?"

Amanda loosened the reins and clicked her tongue. "I would love to," she called over her shoulder as Ebony surged ahead.

SEBASTIAN WATCHED Jocelyn and his sister kick their horses into a gallop and envied them. Goldrush started, as if he would chase after them, but Sebastian held the horse steady.

The earl harrumphed. "That is no way for a lady of quality to ride."

"You're wrong, Father."

"I am not wrong."

Sebastian took a breath and released it. He longed to challenge his father to try riding sidesaddle himself for a day before judging the women for choosing not to do so.

"Lord Hooke," William said, as if attempting to save Sebastian from himself. "I'm not sure what all you'd like to see. I trust Sebastian told you we've got over nine thousand acres for grazing land here on Eden's Gate.

The main part of our herd is up north right now." He pointed. "Closer to the mountains and the creek that runs out of them. We don't have much trouble with creeks running dry in this part of the country. Most years the snowpack stays around well into spring and early summer. We benefit from the runoff."

"What is the size of your herd?"

"About four thousand cows and heifers at this time. About three thousand calves."

"I had no idea."

Sebastian hid a smile. At least something about America had impressed his father.

William continued, "You'll be able to see the cattle once we get up to that ridge. Where Amanda and Jocelyn are headed."

The earl's scowl returned.

As he'd done earlier, Sebastian wished away the days until his wedding would take place.

———

ALTHOUGH TWILIGHT LINGERED past nine o'clock at this time of the year, the entire household had retired well before darkness arrived, everyone exhausted by the tour of the ranch and the tension that stretched between the earl and his son.

When Jocelyn opened the door about half an hour after entering her bedroom, the only sound to be heard was the ticking of the mantle clock in the parlor. She held her breath as she descended the stairs, avoiding the center of the third step from the bottom, the one that often creaked beneath one's weight. Moments later, she stepped onto the front porch and released her breath.

After settling onto a chair, she stared toward the east, the mountains now little more than dark shadows against the darker gray of the sky. A horse huffed and stomped a hoof in one of the corrals. A foal called to its dam, receiving a nicker in reply. Somewhere nearby— perhaps underneath the porch—a dog whimpered in its sleep.

Lord, I felt the earl's disapproval all day long, no matter what I did or said. He doesn't like me. He doesn't think I'm suitable to marry Sebastian. Was I wrong to say yes? Did I agree to marry Sebastian because You opened that door or was I being selfish? I love him. I don't want to lose him. Is that wrong of me?

In the space of her prayer, the gray of the sky had turned to the color of ink. Stars twinkled against the black canvas, seeming to multiply as the seconds passed.

Sebastian seems determined that our wedding will take place despite his father's opposition. Is that because he wants to defy his father or does he defy his father because he truly wants to marry me?

It wasn't too late to change her mind. She could return to New York. She could go back to the business of running Overstreet Shipping. Or she could settle on the ranch with William. She could help run Eden's Gate more efficiently. Then the earl could find a wife for Sebastian who would know what was expected of a future countess.

A countess.

She covered her face with her hands. "What was I thinking?"

"About what?" Sebastian asked from behind her.

She gasped as she jumped up from the chair, her pulse racing. Or perhaps it raced in anticipation. They hadn't been alone, just the two of them, the entire day.

"Sorry," he said. "Didn't mean to startle you."

She wished she could look into his eyes, but it was too dark to see them clearly.

"Do you want to be alone, Jocelyn?"

Her pulse began to slow. "No."

"What *were* you thinking? Or was that a question for God?"

"Perhaps."

He stepped closer, close enough she felt the warmth of his body through his shirt.

"Sebastian, what if your father never approves of me?" She pressed her forehead against his chest.

His arms came around her. "He will. In time."

"But time is something he doesn't have."

"No." There was pain in that single word.

"I'm sorry, Sebastian. I know what it is like to lose a father after already losing a mother."

He kissed the crown of her head, then pressed his cheek against the same spot.

Jocelyn breathed in, wishing she could remain silent but needing to say more. "Even if he had time, I doubt your father would change his mind about me."

"How can he help it, once he gets to know you?"

Doubts welled within, threatening to swamp her. "What about your brother and his wife? Will they approve of our marriage? What of your friends? Do they think like your father?"

Sebastian tightened his arms around her. "Don't do this, Jocelyn. Don't let fear and doubt overtake you. Don't be driven like a wave of the sea. Remember what the Scriptures tell us. 'A double minded man is unstable in all his ways.'"

She wanted to agree with him. She wanted to ignore the doubts and to avoid being double minded. But it wasn't that easy, was it?

She drew back and looked up at him. If only she could see his eyes and command him to tell her he loved her. If he loved her, surely the doubts would go away.

Chapter Twenty-Two

"Sebastian," his father said at breakfast the following morning. "I must send a telegram. Is that possible in this remote place?"

Sebastian inhaled and fought against the tension that tightened the muscles in his shoulders. "Of course it is possible, Father. There's a telegraph office in Gibeon." He would have added something about the cable he'd sent to England a few days earlier, but that would have been a waste of time. His father hadn't received it anyway. "If you write down what you want to say, we can have one of the men ride into town and send it for you."

"No, thank you. I would like to go myself."

Now it was tempting to suggest his father might want to rest after spending so many hours on horseback yesterday. But he was wise enough not to give in to the urge. "Then I'll take you myself. It will give me a chance to show you around Gibeon."

"I don't imagine there is much to see."

True enough. Gibeon was much like many small towns in the American West. A church that served as a school during the week. A restaurant. A doctor's office on the ground floor of the doctor's home. A boarding house instead of a hotel. A couple of saloons. A sheriff's office. A blacksmith and stables. A general store. A post office. A butcher shop. Homes scattered here and there.

The earl would not be impressed.

"I can have the horse and buggy ready to go in half an hour," Sebastian said. "Will that suit you?"

"It will."

Amanda swept into the room, a smile on her face. "What are we doing today?" She paused and gave their father's cheek a peck, then took her plate from the table and went to the sideboard.

"I'm driving Father into Gibeon. He wants to send a telegram."

"Wonderful." His sister dished eggs and biscuits onto her plate. "I'll come too."

Sebastian wasn't sure if Amanda's presence would help or hurt. On one hand, he would like to avoid more disagreements, and Amanda was an excellent buffer most of the time. On the other hand, he might not be able to speak as freely as he wanted if she were with them.

He glanced toward the dining room entrance, wondering if Jocelyn would join them. And did he want her to join them? Not really. Last night, as they'd stood together in the dark, as he'd held her in his arms, she'd seemed fragile, breakable. He'd never seen her that way before. From almost the first moment they met, he'd admired her strength, her confidence, her determination. Where had those qualities gone last night?

Looking toward his father, he thought, *You took them from her.*

Hot resentment welled in his chest. An unfamiliar feeling. Not that he hadn't butted heads with the earl in the past. Many times in fact. Father and son had often differed in their thinking. They'd argued, sometimes vehemently. But this feeling was different. Stronger than anger. An overwhelming desire to protect and shelter Jocelyn, no matter what he had to do.

He pushed his chair back from the table and rose. "I'll be ready to leave in half an hour."

Outside, he selected a horse from the corral and gave it a good grooming, hoping with each stroke of the brush, each flick of the hoof pick, to eliminate the fire inside of him. And it worked to a degree. His anger began to cool and his thoughts became clearer.

Jocelyn hadn't accepted Sebastian's proposal at first. In fact, she'd fled the dining room without answering. She'd needed more than a night to think about it. She'd needed time to talk to the reverend and pray. Even after she'd agreed to marry him, he'd felt the tentativeness in her kisses and had seen it in her eyes. He'd thought it was because she was inexperienced with men, but perhaps it was uncertainty about marrying him at all. Perhaps she hadn't needed his father's disapproval to make her doubt.

He had to face facts. It wasn't only his father's scowls that had shaken Jocelyn's confidence. Why hadn't he understood that? Why hadn't he done more to reassure her? He'd told her they would face challenges. He'd acknowledged she would be a stranger in England and to the ways of the peerage. He'd promised to protect and guide her. But what had he done to continue to bolster her? To begin to prepare her for a new life? Nothing except kiss her whenever the opportunity arose. Was that enough?

"No," he answered aloud. "It's not."

Which brought his thoughts back to his father. It wasn't enough to stand up to the earl. If they were fighting with each other, if anger was all that remained between them, things could only get worse.

A memory of his mother came to him. Her cool hand brushing hair off his forehead as he lay on his bed. Her voice soft and low as she said, *"'Be ye angry, and sin not: let not the sun go down upon your wrath.'"*

It would be nice to know how to obey that command. Be angry but don't sin. Never go to bed angry. Easy to understand. Not so easy to achieve.

He drew in a breath and released it. "Jocelyn shouldn't have to win Father's approval. She isn't the problem. We are. My father and I."

God, show me what to do. Teach me what to say.

SEBASTIAN HAD to marvel at his sister's ability to read his mood. How else would she have known to back out of the trip into Gibeon at the last moment?

"You go ahead," Amanda had told him while he stood with the horse and buggy, waiting for the earl to come out of the house. "You need time to talk with Father without others around. I'll spend the day with Jocelyn."

The morning was already warm as the two men set out in the buggy. Neither of them spoke for the first ten minutes or so. Which was fine with Sebastian as he wrestled with what he might say and what he hoped the results to be.

It was his father who broke the silence at last. "It's all rather barren out here."

Sebastian knew from his own trips to and from town over the past two months that the ranch house had disappeared from view behind them. And ahead of them, Gibeon was hidden by the rolling countryside. "I thought so, too, at first. But I don't see it that way anymore."

"Hmm."

"From here you can see mountain ranges in almost every direction." He jerked his head to indicate the peaks off to their right. "Nothing like them in England."

"No. That is true. But I don't understand why you remain so enamored with this blasted country. You're an Englishman. Why doesn't your own country satisfy you?"

Sebastian took a breath, fighting to remain calm, resisting the anger that came so quickly with his father. "I love England, sir. Surely you know that. But I don't understand why you resent my interest in the American West. You didn't object when I went to Egypt or the French Alps or the Mediterranean Sea."

"It isn't the country I object to. It's the people.

Americans are brash, assertive, lacking in refinement. They're an uncivilized lot."

"The Overstreets aren't uncivilized."

The earl harrumphed. "Well, perhaps not them. After all, William went to school in England, and I suppose Miss Overstreet must have been exposed to some refined culture while living in New York, even if she doesn't ride like a lady."

Sebastian wanted to grind his teeth.

"But I'll be bound, the men who work on the ranch are just as I suspect." His father punctuated the comment with a firm nod of his chin. "Rough and uncivilized, like this land."

"Have you taken the time to speak to any of those men? To find out who they are and what they are actually like."

His father looked at Sebastian as if he'd sprouted a second head.

"That's what I thought. You judge them without knowing them."

"I know what I see."

"Did you take the time to speak to Jocelyn before you deemed her unworthy to be my wife? No, you judged her out of hand as well."

His father appeared irritated. But then the frown altered slightly, as if he were giving his son's questions and comments some consideration.

Sebastian clucked his tongue and slapped the reins against the horse's backside and allowed the silence to return between them.

WHILE THEIR HORSES grazed in the shade of the pines and aspens, Jocelyn sat beside Amanda on a rock ledge, their bare feet dangling in the frigid waters tumbling out of the mountains. Despite the heat of midday, Jocelyn grew chilled in a hurry. She pulled her feet out of the rushing stream and hugged her legs to her chest. Amanda soon did the same.

"I cannot believe the water is that cold when the day so warm," Amanda said.

"There's a pool a little higher up the mountain." Jocelyn looked in that direction. "Sometimes the men go there for a swim, but it's always been too cold for me. This water was snow and ice just a few days ago." She scooted back on the rock and lay down, staring skyward. "I needed this. I'm glad we came."

"It's truly wonderful. Thank you for sharing it with me."

"Billy and I used to ride up here a lot when we were children. We weren't ever supposed to come without an adult, but once we did. We escaped getting caught, but my conscience bothered me afterward, and I determined I wouldn't disobey Mama's rules again." She smiled at the memory. "Then Billy went off to school in England, and I didn't care to come without him, even with another adult. It just wasn't the same without him."

Amanda lay down beside Jocelyn. "Why isn't William married?"

Jocelyn rolled her head to the side to look at her. "Why? Have you formed an attachment with him?"

The younger woman's only response was to laugh.

"I'm serious."

"So am I," Amanda replied, still chuckling.

Jocelyn felt herself stiffen. "What's wrong with my brother?"

Amanda sobered at once. "Nothing is wrong with him. I like William a lot. But I feel about him the same way I feel about my two brothers. And I rather think he sees me more like a sister. I asked because you and Sebastian will go to England after you're married, and Roger and I are only staying until spring. I hate to think of your brother rattling around by himself in that big house once everyone is gone."

"He doesn't seem to mind." As soon as Jocelyn said the words, she questioned them. Perhaps William minded more than she knew. Maybe more than he knew. Loneliness could be the reason the ranch accounts had been in such disarray. Maybe he hated being in his office with no one else around. "Do I need to worry about him?"

"No, you don't. Worry solves nothing. That is what my mother used to say to my brothers. She liked to remind them of that verse in the Bible that tells us not to worry."

Jocelyn smiled at a memory. "My mother said the same."

"I am confident they would have liked each other. Our mothers."

"Perhaps your mother would have liked me, too."

"Oh, Jocelyn. She would have adored you." Amanda rolled onto her side, facing Jocelyn, and tucked her arm beneath her head. "She would have loved you because Sebastian loves you."

Jocelyn's breath caught. *Does he love me?* She wished she had the courage to ask the question aloud. Instead she drew in a breath and said, "Tell me about your mother."

"I don't remember much. I was only five when she died. Sometimes I'm not sure what I actually remember and what I think I remember because of what my brothers have told me. I know that she was kind to all, from nobility to the lowest servant. Sebastian says my laugh is like hers, and Father says my smile is the same. She had a strong faith in God. I remember her kneeling beside my bed with me and teaching me to pray."

"I'm sorry you didn't have more years with her."

Amanda swallowed and blinked, as if fighting tears. "So do I."

Hoping to turn her friend's thoughts to something less sad, she said, "Now tell me about Hooke Manor."

"What would you like to know?"

"Anything. Whatever you would like me to know."

Amanda seemed to brighten a little. "Well, the manor is quite large, of course. The Overstreet house is impressive, but nothing like the ancestral seat of the Earl of Hooke. The manor is four stories tall, including the top floor where the servant rooms are located, plus there's an attic above those rooms. In all, the manor has about forty bedchambers on the second and third floors. Actually, I believe it is forty-five bedchambers."

"Forty-five?" The picture of the manor Jocelyn had formed in her mind abruptly changed.

"Mmm. On the main floor there's the grand saloon and a long, beautiful drawing room. There's a dining room with a table that seats forty with room to spare. There is the music room with the Steinway grand as its focal point and the morning room that my mother particularly favored. There are many other rooms besides, including two libraries. Hooke Manor doesn't have a ballroom, but we have hosted some wonderful balls using the grand saloon and drawing room combined. We had a house party with dancing earlier this year. That was where Adam proposed to Eliza, despite her father's objections."

"Do *all* fathers in England object to the marriages of their children?"

Amanda laughed. "No. But Eliza's father wanted her to marry Sebastian, the future earl, not his half-brother. Adam will never have a title and won't inherit any of the Whitcombe estates. Neither he nor Eliza care about that, of course. They are quite happy in their cottage."

"Back to the bedrooms." Jocelyn tried to picture the place where she was supposed to live as Sebastian's wife. Forty-five bedrooms? That was more like a castle or even a hotel in New York City. It didn't sound like a home for a single family. "Do you ever have a need for that many sleeping rooms?"

"Not in my lifetime. Perhaps a hundred years ago, before the railroad. Back then, people came to visit and stayed for weeks at a time. Still, we have had house parties where at least twenty-five of the bedchambers were occupied and the guests remained for a week or more."

A house party for so many and that lasted so long? Dread snaked around Jocelyn's heart.

I'm not suitable. Just as the earl says.

Chapter Twenty-Three

The earl sent two telegrams that morning. One went to Adam in England. The other went to his valet at a hotel in New York. Sebastian didn't know what either telegram said and didn't ask. He was content to wait just inside the telegraph office near the door.

As the two men stepped onto the boardwalk after the messages had been sent, his father asked, "Does Gibeon have a physician?"

"Are you feeling all right? Do I need to take you back to the ranch?"

"I am fine at the moment. But I find I must arrange for more of my medications. I seem to have left some behind with Hughes."

Sebastian wondered what his father required. Since he had cancer, a cancer that was killing him, he probably needed laudanum to control the pain. What else might he need? And could Dr. Grant help him?

Sebastian's throat ached with sudden emotion. He and the earl hadn't had a detailed discussion about his

235

father's health, about his pain and any other symptoms, and that was as much his fault as his father's. "Dr. Grant has an office at the end of the street." He pointed to the house on the western edge of town. "We'll go there now."

With a soft grunt, his father stepped up into the buggy. Sebastian rounded the back of the vehicle to do the same. In moments, he'd turned the horse and buggy toward Dr. Grant's home and office.

"You will like Dr. Grant, Father. He took excellent care of William after he was injured and did the same for Amanda when she was ill."

"Your sister was ill?" His father glared at him. "Why wasn't I told? When was that?"

"Almost two weeks ago, and it only lasted a short while. It wasn't worth mentioning. You had much more serious things to tell us. Remember?"

"Anything could go wrong in this wilderness you brought Amanda to."

"Anything could go wrong back in England as well." The moment the words were out of his mouth, he wished he could take them back. He needed to heed the words of Jesus and be a peacemaker.

Easier said than done with his father.

At the doctor's house, Sebastian tied the horse to a hitching rail, then waited for his father to get out of the buggy and lead the way up the walk to the front porch. A sign on the wall read, *Oxford Grant, Physician*. The earl grunted, as if to dispute the claim. A second, smaller sign said, *Enter*.

When they went inside, a bell above the door

chimed. The front parlor had been turned into a waiting area, but no other patients were in the room at present. Before they could be seated, a middle-aged woman in a dark dress and white apron appeared in a doorway.

"May I help you?" she asked with an encouraging smile.

"I am Sebastian Whitcombe. My father would like to see Dr. Grant."

Just then the doctor himself appeared in another doorway. "Mr. Whitcombe. Is all well at the ranch?"

"Yes." He glanced toward the earl. "Father, this is Dr. Grant. Dr. Grant, may I introduce my father, Lord Hooke. He needs to consult with you, if you have the time."

"Of course." The doctor offered a hand to the earl to shake. "Lord Hooke, it's a pleasure to make your acquaintance. Come into my office and you can tell me your concerns."

Sebastian wanted to go with the other two men, but the look his father shot his way told him he wouldn't be welcome. He sat on one of the waiting room chairs instead and prayed Dr. Grant could give his father the help he needed.

Time dragged by. A clock on the wall counted the passing of seconds, although the cadence sounded too slow in Sebastian's ears. The nurse—or at least he assumed the woman they'd met earlier was a nurse—moved about the adjoining room, opening a drawer, putting something in a cabinet, straightening a stack of papers. But even her movements seemed to be slower than what was normal.

His father, the Earl of Hooke was dying. Perhaps in a matter of months or even weeks. His father had come to America because he believed it would be sooner rather than later. Little time remained for him to force his son to obey him. Little time for Sebastian to win his father's approval as well.

He stood and walked to the window to stare out at the quiet street leading through Gibeon.

He couldn't obey his father when it came to Jocelyn. He couldn't and wouldn't. He'd made his decision. He knew who he wanted to marry. He wasn't wrong about Jocelyn Overstreet. She was the right woman for him. It wasn't merely her beauty, although he thought her beautiful. It wasn't merely her intelligence, although he found her bright as well. It wasn't her zest for life, which he'd seen so often. It wasn't only that he desired her—and he did desire her. More so with every passing day. Instead, it was something he knew deep in his heart. He believed God had brought him to Idaho to meet her.

Now You need to change Father's mind about her, Lord. You need to change his heart.

Last night, he'd quoted from the book of James, telling Jocelyn not to give in to her fears and doubts, telling her not to be double minded. Now it was time to quote a different passage from James, this time to himself. For that verse told him to ask God for wisdom.

And if anyone needed wisdom, it was surely Sebastian Whitcombe.

Jocelyn and Amanda rode away from the cascading mountain stream as the sun passed its zenith. Even before they'd left the shade of the trees, they forgot how frozen their feet had felt when dangling in the cold, rushing waters.

"I'm not used to this heat," Amanda said, frowning up at the cloudless sky from beneath the brim of her hat. "It never gets this hot in England. Not where we live."

"It's much worse in New York than here. At the ranch, on this side of the Rockies, you can stand in the shade and find immediate relief. We're over five thousand feet above sea level here." Jocelyn tugged her hat lower on her forehead. "But I agree. It's miserably hot today."

"Poor Sebastian."

"Why poor Sebastian?"

"Because Father has probably blamed him for the heat on their trip back from Gibeon."

"Would he do that?"

Amanda chuckled. "He would say it, whether or not he meant it. He tends to grumble about things and put the blame on others when he's uncomfortable. Still, his bark is worse than his bite, as people say."

Jocelyn thought of her own father. He'd known how to be strong and assertive with the men who worked at Overstreet Shipping. He'd known how to be firm with his children, too, and had disciplined them as required. But he'd also been a kind man. She couldn't imagine him blaming William for the heat of summer. And she couldn't imagine him telling a woman he didn't yet know that she was unsuitable to marry his son.

How quickly her thoughts returned to Sebastian and their plans to marry, to the earl's disapproval of her, and to the England she'd never seen.

She closed her eyes. *God, I keep going round and round in my mind. I don't know what to do.*

Almost as if Amanda had heard the prayer, she said, "I wish I could help."

Jocelyn looked over at her.

"I wish I could help you regain your confidence."

"What do you mean?"

"Isn't it obvious?" The younger woman's smile was sweet . . . and a little sad. "You aren't the same person you were in May. I thought . . . Well, you seemed so sure of yourself when we first met. You were so confident and fearless. When I watched you ride, I saw your joy. You were happy." She paused, then added, "I always thought falling in love made a girl happier than ever before."

"I thought so too," Jocelyn whispered.

"You do love Sebastian, don't you?"

She closed her eyes a second time, letting the question swirl around inside her mind, testing her reaction to it. After a long while, she looked over at Amanda. "Yes, I love him. But I wonder if that is enough."

They were silent for the remainder of the ride back to the ranch.

Chapter Twenty-Four

Word of rustlers hitting several ranches to the south of Eden's Gate had all the cowboys —William and Sebastian included—mounted up early on Saturday morning and riding in three directions to protect the Overstreet cattle and help their neighbors.

Standing on the porch, Jocelyn watched the men ride away, part of her wishing she'd ridden out with them. She could have. William wouldn't have stopped her, and Sebastian would have welcomed her. But something told her she should stay behind, that she still had answers to find and she wouldn't find them out on the range. She needed to find them within.

With all the cowboys and most of the horses gone, the barnyard seemed eerily silent. Even the chickens in the coop chose not to cluck.

Jocelyn stepped off the porch and made her way to the barn. As she went through the wide doorway, a barn cat hissed at her from the shadows on her right. The cat jumped to the top rail of a stall, then climbed until it reached the hayloft. There, it sat and began to bathe itself, as if it had never been bothered by her entrance.

Oh, for her own peace to return that quickly.

She continued to Bella's stall where she dropped hay into the feed box. After that she carried the bucket to the pump and filled it to the brim before returning it to the stall. Then she stood at the railing and watched the horse eat while letting her thoughts drift to the previous day.

Nothing had seemed right after she and Amanda returned to the ranch house. Sebastian and his father had already been there, and the older man had closed himself away in his room for the remainder of the day. Sebastian might as well have done the same, for he had been uncommunicative, settling for one word answers to any questions sent his way at the supper table. Later, he'd sat with an open book on his lap for the majority of the evening.

She should release Sebastian. She should tell him it was better for them not to marry. Better for them both. His father was against the union, and the thought nagged at her: Maybe the earl was right. Even though she loved Sebastian. Did that make her double minded?

When Bella had cleaned the last of the hay from the feed box, Jocelyn led the mare out of the barn and placed her in a nearby paddock, along with Red and two other geldings. Bella stayed near the gate for a while, perhaps hoping for more hay or an apple or carrot.

Jocelyn shook her head and chuckled as she gave the

mare's neck a pat. "Nothing more for you, girl." She turned and walked to the house.

Voices from the dining room told her Amanda and her father had come down for breakfast. She drew a deep breath to steel herself before walking in that direction.

"Jocelyn!" Amanda greeted her with enthusiasm. "There you are. Mrs. Adler said all the men have ridden out for today. I was starting to wonder if you went with them."

"No. I decided to remain behind."

"Good, because Mrs. Adler needs some help with your dress."

The earl glanced up from his breakfast plate, frowned at his daughter, and looked down again.

Her dress. Mrs. Adler had insisted she wanted to make Jocelyn a wedding dress. Something more appropriate for a viscountess than what Jocelyn wore to work in the city, or even to church on Sundays. Certainly something more appropriate than the split skirt she wore around the ranch the rest of the week.

More appropriate. Did dear Mrs. Adler have a clue what a viscountess was or what type of clothes one would wear? Doubtful. But then, Jocelyn didn't know either. Except that even the everyday attire must be more grand than anything she had in her wardrobe. But if she broke off the engagement, there was no need for a new dress. Should she say as much to the housekeeper before she wasted time on a dress that would never be worn?

Jocelyn took a plate to the sideboard and added

some food to it. Afterward, she returned to her place at the table and sat. She said a silent prayer of thanks before placing a cloth napkin on her lap.

"Miss Overstreet."

She looked at the earl, nerves jangling. When was the last time he'd addressed her directly? The day of his arrival perhaps. "Yes, my lord."

"Might we sit and talk awhile this morning, you and I?"

She folded her hands in her lap, squeezing hard. "If you wish, sir."

"It would be wise, I believe."

"Of course." Her answer sounded calm and composed, but what she wanted was to sprint from the room, to run away and hide.

Why am I behaving like this? I've encountered more disagreeable men than Lord Hooke.

Perhaps that thought wasn't true, but she told herself it was. She had to if she was going to feel strong enough to talk with him alone. Even if she ultimately decided she wouldn't marry his son.

FOR MORE THAN AN HOUR, William, Sebastian, Rocky Turner, and Tom Flores rode in silence, their gazes sweeping the land ahead of them, looking for signs of trouble. Not that Sebastian knew what such a sign would be. He'd helped move Eden's Gate cattle from one grazing area to another many times over the last couple of months, but he wouldn't be able to tell if any of the cattle were missing.

"Hey, boss!" Rocky called. The cowboy had ridden up on a ridge and was looking through a pair of binoculars. "Looks like we might have some fence down along the south pasture."

William joined Rocky, then motioned for Sebastian and Tom to follow them. After a slow descent on the other side of the ridge, the four men nudged their horses into a canter. Sebastian allowed the others to lead the way while he brought up the rear.

It was obvious, upon arrival, that the barbed wire had been cut before being stretched back out of the way.

Rocky dismounted and hovered his fingers over the ground. "I'd say six or seven horses, boss, but it doesn't look like any cattle have gone out this way." He stood and looked west. "They rode in that direction. Could still be on your land."

"And if they're not here," William said, his voice hard, "we can be sure they'll cut their way through another section of fence farther down the line. Let's ride."

Rocky swung into his saddle, and they took off again, this time at a gallop.

Sebastian felt the urgency in his bones. After two months on the ranch—not to mention the day he'd spent helping Jocelyn reorganize the account books—he understood what the loss of cattle could do to Eden's Gate's bottom line. Whether William lost cattle to a hungry grizzly bear or lost them to thieves or sickness or weather, the end result was the same. Fewer cattle to sell to the buyers come round up time. Less income for the ranch to sustain them through the coming year.

When he saw William pull his rifle from the scabbard on the saddle, he prepared to do the same. But then he saw William slide the rifle back in its place. "It's Luke Fisher and his men," William called to the others. In unison, they slowed their horses to a canter, then a trot.

Sweat trickled down Sebastian's spine, and he knew it had as much to do with the excitement he'd felt— along with a rush of dread—as from the heat.

Approaching the five other men, William greeted his neighboring rancher. 'Luke."

"William. You got word of the rustlers?"

"Yeah. Been out since right after dawn." He jerked his head, indicating the way they'd come. "Got some fence down back that way. Wire's been cut."

"You'll find more of the same about a quarter mile back. We were looking for tracks when we came across the open fence."

"They hit you?"

"Three nights ago. A couple hundred head gone, best I can tell. Could be more."

William gave a grim nod. "We followed tracks this way. If there's more fence cut, looks like it was their exit."

Luke rubbed his forehead with the fingers of one hand. "You might've got lucky then. We saw no signs of cattle going through back there. Maybe they saw you comin' and made themselves scarce."

William's gaze swept the terrain. "I plan to stay lucky. You do the same, Luke."

With a tip of his hat, Luke Fisher rode off with his men in the direction of the downed fence.

William turned his horse to face his own men. "Rocky, we'll need to get the wire repaired. You'll be in charge of that."

"Yes, boss."

"Tom, I want all the cattle brought to the pastures east of the ranch house. We'll keep our boys out there night and day. Jake can hire on more men if needed. Find him and let him know."

"Yes, sir." Tom didn't wait to hear more instructions. He jabbed his mount in the sides. The horse leapt into a gallop. With a nod toward William, Rocky followed right after Tom.

Goldrush pranced in place, eager to take off after the other horses. "Easy, boy." Sebastian kept a firm grip on the reins.

"When I invited you to come and stay," William said, "I never envisioned this kind of summer. A rogue bison. A grizzly bear on the range. Now rustlers."

Hoping to lighten the mood, Sebastian replied, "Not to mention me proposing to your sister."

William's grunt held no humor.

Sebastian sobered. "What can I do to help?"

"Rocky will make sure the fence is repaired. You and I need to help move the cattle."

"Jocelyn will want to help. Amanda too."

"Then we'd better go get them."

AFTER MORE THAN an hour in her bedroom with Mrs. Adler, trying on the dress and waiting for it to be pinned here and there, Jocelyn made her way downstairs and out to the porch, arriving at the appointed time. The earl was there before her.

"I hope you haven't been waiting long, Lord Hooke."

He didn't look at her. "I have little else to do but wait."

As she settled onto a chair, she wondered if he referred to the return of Sebastian or to the cancer growing in his stomach.

"Miss Overstreet." He waited for her to meet his gaze. "I love my son."

"I'm sure you do, sir."

"Are you sure? I am not convinced Sebastian believes it."

Was this why he'd wanted to talk, the two of them? Did he want her to speak to Sebastian on his behalf? That seemed unlikely.

"He believes I have been unfair to you." The earl reached for a glass of lemonade and took a sip. He grimaced as he set the glass back onto the small table beside him. "Perhaps I have been. But there is no time for mistakes."

"And you believe I'm a mistake."

He grimaced a second time, his hand going to his belly.

"Is there something I can get you, Lord Hooke?"

She leaned toward him. "Something to make you more comfortable?"

"There is nothing." He drew in a breath and released it. "Miss Overstreet, why do you wish to marry my son?"

She leaned against the back of the chair. "There are many reasons."

"Are there?"

"Yes."

"For his wealth?"

She stiffened. "No. That is not important to me. I have money of my own." Never mind it was likely a fraction of the earl's.

"For his title?"

She shook her head. "No."

"Are you saying the title isn't important, young woman?"

Jocelyn saw the trap the earl was setting and hoped she could avoid it. But *should* she avoid it? If she was conflicted about marrying Sebastian, even though she loved him, perhaps she should let the earl win. But honesty wouldn't allow it.

"Lord Hooke, while a title isn't important to me, it *is* important to Sebastian. He is your heir, and he is proud of it. He doesn't *need* the title, mind you, but he understands the responsibilities that come with it." She drew a breath. "I would marry your son because he's a caring and trustworthy man. He is smart and incredibly hardworking. He is honorable and giving. While I don't understand everything an earldom requires of the man who inherits the title, I do understand that Sebastian will do all he can to bring honor to the title and the family name."

"You have learned all of that in such a short time?"

"I have, my lord."

"You defend the boy better than he defends himself."

"Sebastian is hardly a boy, sir. And does he need to defend himself?"

The earl gave her a long, piercing look. "You have a fire in you, Miss Overstreet."

"Do I, Lord Hooke?"

Whatever he might have replied was interrupted by the return of some of the cowboys, Sebastian among them. Amidst the commotion, the earl must have retired into the house, for when she turned back, Jocelyn saw that he'd disappeared, putting an end to their conversation.

Chapter Twenty-Five

It took the better part of the next three days for the Eden's Gate men—along with Jocelyn and Amanda —to drive all the cattle from the various grazing areas to the pastures immediately to the east of the ranch house. Once there, the cowboys kept a close watch on the herd, both day and night. More men from ranches to the west and south searched the region for the rustlers and stolen cattle. So far they'd come up empty handed.

"This really is the Wild West," Amanda said as she and Sebastian watched the sheriff and several deputies ride out of the barnyard on Tuesday morning.

"Seems that way."

William walked back to join them in the shade of the porch.

"Any signs of the rustlers?" Sebastian asked.

"None. It's like they vanished into thin air."

"I suppose if they've left the area that's good news."

William gave his head a slight shake. "Doesn't make me feel any better. They got away with a lot of cattle between the several ranches they hit. Could make them greedy and willing to try for more." With another shake of the head, he left them and strode to his horse, mounted, and rode off toward the herd and the men watching them.

Sebastian wondered if he should follow William. No, better to remain behind. The last three days had been busy ones, and he'd spent almost no time with his father or Jocelyn. Perhaps he didn't mind so much about his father, but not being with Jocelyn left him frustrated. He suspected she'd been avoiding time alone with him. That thought made him frown.

"Look," Amanda interrupted. "Here comes another visitor."

Sebastian followed the direction of her gaze and watched the approach of a wagon with two men on the driver's seat.

"By Jove!" he said as the wagon rolled into the yard. "It's Roger."

Roger called to them, "I say, it's good to be back." He dropped to the ground after the wagon stopped. He looked hot and unkempt, but he wore a wide grin. "Amanda, my dear, you look in the pink of health. I'm thankful to see it."

His sister hurried off the porch and went to give Roger a hug. "I am well." As soon as she stepped back from his embrace, she added, "But we didn't expect you for two more days. You must tell us all about the park. Is it as wonderful as we've heard? How many paintings did you return with? I want to see them all."

"Give him a moment, Amanda. Let him catch his

breath." Sebastian joined his sister. "It is good to have you back, my friend. We wish we could have joined you on your adventure in Yellowstone."

Amanda continued as if she hadn't been interrupted. "We've had adventures of a different kind. You won't believe all that's happened here. First of all, Father arrived last week."

"What?" Roger turned a surprised gaze on Sebastian. "Am I hearing things?"

"No."

"The earl is here? In America." Roger looked toward the house. "He's here *now*?"

"Yes."

"But that's not all." Amanda looked back and forth between the two men. "Sebastian is getting married."

Roger shook his head. "I don't believe it. You were supposed to have another year before you looked for a wife. Is this your father's doing?"

Amanda laughed. "Far from it."

Sebastian sent a warning glance at his sister. "I asked Miss Overstreet to marry me."

"And she said yes," Amanda interjected, "and they will marry in less than two weeks."

Roger took a half-step back. "By heaven, that is a surprise."

"It was a surprise to Father, too." As soon as the words were out, Amanda's smile vanished. She sucked in a quick breath, then whirled away and hurried into the house.

An unspoken question entered Roger's eyes.

Sebastian answered it. "Father has cancer. He may

not have long to live, according to the physicians in England. Perhaps a few months."

"I am sorry, old man. That is difficult news. I . . . I am horribly sorry."

He nodded, his throat suddenly tight.

Roger turned and looked up at the wagon driver. "Thank you for allowing me to ride along with you, Mr. Jones. Could we offer some refreshment before you continue on your way?"

"No, sir. I'm right as rain. Got everything I need and not that much farther to go. Been my pleasure havin' your company. Made the miles go by faster to have somebody to talk to."

Sebastian went to the back of the wagon with Roger and helped unload the canvases wrapped in burlap, along with the easel, other art supplies, and one carpet bag. Once everything was unloaded, Mr. Jones drove his wagon out of the barnyard.

Still holding two bundles of canvases, Sebastian said, "Let's get all this out of the sun. Then I'll take you in to see Father."

JOCELYN SAT on the edge of the bed, listening to the muffled voices coming from the parlor downstairs.

In her hands, she held a letter from Paul Danvers, her assistant at Overstreet Shipping. One of the cowboys had returned from town with the letter only a short while ago. Paul had written to advise her of some of the decisions the board had made during her absence. Jocelyn agreed with most of them but questioned a few. For instance, she didn't agree there was need for a new ship to be built for the Mediterranean route. Had the board considered taking a ship from a less profitable route? If she had been there—

But she hadn't been in the Overstreet Shipping boardroom when that decision was made, and she wouldn't be in those offices again. Not for any length of time. After her marriage, she would move to England. She would have an entirely different life than the one she'd known for so many years. And William had no more interest in the shipping company now than he'd had before their father died.

That was why she and William had decided to appoint someone to officially fill her role at the company for the next year. At the end of that time, the two of them would decide if they wanted to sell the company or if they would remain owners from a distance. But selling seemed the preferable option.

Sell Overstreet Shipping.

She rose from the bed and walked to the dresser. On it sat a framed photograph of her father, taken a couple of years before his death. His beard had turned a pale gray by that time, obvious even in a black and white photograph. He'd worn a serious expression, as was common when one had to hold still for a lengthy period of time. Oh, but she missed his smiling face. She wished that smile could have been captured for her to look at again and again.

"What would you tell us to do, Papa?" She smiled sadly. "What would you think about Sebastian? What would you think of me marrying a viscount and moving to England? Would you be happy for me? Or would you tell me to call it off, to return to New York, to continue with the life I've made for myself."

A knock at her door interrupted her musing. She turned to face it. "Enter."

The door opened and Amanda looked in. "Did you know Roger is back from the park?"

"No. I didn't." She folded the letter and set it on the dresser next to her father's photograph. "He wasn't expected until Thursday."

Amanda opened the door a little wider. She smiled, but it didn't reach her eyes. "He was surprised to hear about you and Sebastian."

"I imagine so."

"And Father. He was surprised to learn Father is here." She sniffed, then placed a handkerchief to her nose.

Jocelyn moved across the room. "Are you quite all right, Amanda?"

"Yes. It just . . . it just hits me in waves sometimes. Knowing that father is so unwell. I forget for a while. Everything seems quite normal. Then suddenly I remember again." She drew a breath. "But I'll be fine, and I refuse to be sad in front of Father."

Jocelyn put her arms around Amanda and held her close. After a short while, Amanda drew back, offered a tremulous smile, and said, "We should join the others."

As Jocelyn followed her friend out of the bedroom, she recalled how upset she'd been by the presence of the Whitcombes and their friend Roger. She hadn't wanted them in the Overstreet family home. And now —dare she say it?—they had become like family. Would it be the same once they were at Hooke Manor? Would they still be like family or would she become an outsider once she reached England's shores?

"Look, Roger," Amanda called at the bottom of the stairs. "Jocelyn has joined us at last."

The three men rose as Jocelyn and Amanda approached the chairs and sofa.

"Miss Overstreet." Roger bowed his head.

"Mr. Bernhardt. I trust the time you spent in the park was everything you hoped for."

"Indeed it was. Yellowstone is even more spectacular than I expected. My only regret is that Amanda and Sebastian weren't able to see it with me. I plan to return this summer, if at all possible."

In unspoken agreement, everyone sat down.

The earl said, "You were telling us of the geysers, Mr. Bernhardt. Please continue."

Roger obliged the request with obvious enthusiasm.

Jocelyn remembered her own visits into the national park, especially the first times she'd seen the geysers and hot springs, the dramatic waterfalls, the beautiful Yellowstone Lake. But never had she heard those places described more eloquently than she heard now. Roger Bernhardt's artist's eye brought the great American wonderland to life in her mind in a new and vibrant way. She couldn't wait to see the paintings he'd done while there.

A grunt scattered the picturesque scenes forming in

her mind. It was followed by a cry of pain. She looked to see the earl bent forward in his chair.

"Father?" Amanda placed a hand on the earl's back, her gaze shooting to Sebastian who was already on his feet.

The earl gasped, tried to straighten, then cried out again.

As Sebastian knelt before his father, he cried, "Send someone for the doctor."

Jocelyn was quick to obey.

Chapter Twenty-Six

I don't need the doctor," Sebastian's father growled as he was helped to his bedroom. A declaration that was clearly untrue.

Sebastian exchanged a look with Roger, and they kept going, half-guiding and half-dragging the older man up the stairs.

As soon as the earl sat on the edge of the bed, he waved toward the nightstand. "My medicine. In that bottle."

Sebastian grabbed the small, dark-glass bottle—laudanum, he was sure—opened it, and held it toward his father. The earl took it, gasped again, then took a quick swallow from the bottle. He paused to draw breath before taking another sip.

"We need to make you comfortable," Sebastian said as he took the bottle from his father's unsteady grasp.

The earl dropped back on the bed, his eyes closed. "Give me a moment. Just give me a moment."

Sebastian returned the laudanum to the nightstand.

"Where's Hughes?" his father mumbled.

"Hughes?" Roger looked at Sebastian.

"His valet." To his father he said, "Hughes isn't with you, Father. Remember?"

"Never could depend upon that man."

Sebastian shook his head slowly. Hughes had served as the earl's valet for as far back as Sebastian could remember. A most reliable man, as the earl well knew.

Roger spoke under his breath. "I was surprised when you left your valet back in England, Sebastian, but I understood why. You wanted the full adventure. But your father doing the same?"

"He didn't do the same. Hughes broke his leg on their way over. Father left him in New York to recover."

"From the look of the earl, he never should have come at all."

"He was determined to see me." Sebastian took a deep breath, then leaned down to remove his father's shoes. After they were off, Roger helped him pull the older man around until his head rested on the pillow and his feet on the mattress.

"Now we wait." Sebastian drew a straight-backed chair up to the bedside.

"I'll go keep watch for the doctor."

"It'll be well over an hour before he gets here."

"I'll keep watch anyway." Roger left the bedroom.

Sebastian wasn't alone for long. Within minutes, the door opened and Amanda entered. She pulled a second chair away from the wall and placed it next to Sebastian.

"He looks ghastly," she whispered into the silence.

He couldn't argue. His father was pale and drawn

and looked much older than he had only yesterday. He'd always seemed indomitable to Sebastian. Not anymore.

Sebastian had mourned and still missed his mother, but he'd never considered his father would die before he was an old, old man. Even after being told about the cancer and prognosis, Sebastian hadn't allowed it to sink in completely. Until now. Until seeing the Earl of Hooke lying here, pallid and unmoving.

He took hold of his sister's hand, and together they awaited the doctor.

***

"Miss Joss." The housekeeper stepped into Jocelyn's path, stopping her pacing. "You'll change nothing by wearing a groove in the floor with your walking to and fro. I'm sure Dr. Grant or Mr. Whitcombe will come down and tell you what you need to know, as soon as they are able."

"It's strange, Mrs. Adler. I don't know why I'm this upset. Lord Hooke has been nothing but disagreeable since he arrived. And he despises the idea of me marrying his son."

"I wouldn't be so sure. I've seen him watching you over the last few days. I believe he's had a change of heart."

Jocelyn shook her head. "I doubt that."

Mrs. Adler stepped closer and took both of her hands, holding them between her own. "I am not wrong. He's changed his opinion about you, same as I changed mine about Mr. Whitcombe."

"I'm glad you changed your mind about Sebastian."

"It wasn't easy, mind you. And I'm not so certain about you going so far away. New York was too far, if you ask me. But England?"

"Maybe we shouldn't marry. Maybe I shouldn't move so far away."

"Mercy, Miss Joss. What a thing to say." The housekeeper reached up and put her fingertips on Jocelyn's cheek. "Of course you should marry him. I've seen the love in your eyes. It reminds me of the way your dear mother always looked at Mr. Overstreet."

"Truly?"

"Truly." Mrs. Adler took her hand away and stepped back, schooling her features into a stern expression. "Don't think I haven't seen your doubts. No. Don't try to deny it. I've seen them. But your doubts aren't about becoming Mrs. Whitcombe. Like I said, you love that man. Your doubts are about yourself, about how you'll measure up. And the earl, bless him, hasn't made it any easier. But don't you let those doubts win. Don't you let the earl's doubts win either, if he's still got any left. You're an Overstreet. You hear me? You keep your head up. You keep your spirits up." She patted her own chest. "You listen to your heart, and you mind what the Spirit is telling you deep inside."

"Thank you for that. It's just that—" Jocelyn looked up toward the earl's bedroom. Sebastian and Amanda were still with their father, along with the doctor who had arrived less than half an hour before. "I hate waiting."

"It's hard on everybody."

As if in answer to Jocelyn's watching eyes, Sebastian stepped into the hallway at the top of the stairs. "My father has asked for you."

"He's asked for me?"

He nodded.

No matter Mrs. Adler's words of encouragement moments before, she felt as if she were walking to the gallows as she climbed the stairs. It could not be a good thing, for her to be summoned to the earl's bedside.

Sebastian waited for her at the top of the stairs, and he immediately took hold of her hand and pressed it against his chest.

"What does he want?"

"I don't know. He simply asked for you to join us."

"He's taken a bad turn, hasn't he?"

Sebastian nodded.

Jocelyn remembered all too well what it had been like for her mother and then her father as they'd let go of their tethers to this mortal world. That had been Mama's description of death, and thinking of it caused tears to spring to Jocelyn's eyes. Neither of her parents had been afraid at the end. They'd been confident in their relationships with their Savior. But the process of dying, her father had said, was rarely an easy journey.

Blinking back the tears, she squeezed Sebastian's hand. "Let's not keep him waiting."

Upon entering the bedroom, Jocelyn took in the scene. The doctor stood near the window, cleaning his eyeglasses with a cloth. Amanda sat by the bed, holding her father's hand. And the earl looked markedly different from the imperious man who had said, only six days before, that Jocelyn was unsuitable to marry his son.

"Miss Overstreet," he whispered.

"I am here." She stepped to the side of the bed, placing one hand on Amanda's shoulder.

The earl grimaced, and his eyes closed again. After taking a breath, he said in a raspy voice, "Do you remember when I said you had a fire in you?"

"Yes."

"Sebastian will need that fire."

Her heart fluttered. "My lord?"

"Sebastian." He opened his eyes. "Come here."

"Yes, Father." Sebastian came to stand beside Jocelyn, and he took her free hand in his.

"I was wrong."

"Sir?"

"I have been wrong about many things." The earl's gaze shifted to Jocelyn. "Your mother would have approved of this girl."

Sebastian's hand tightened its grip on hers. "Yes, sir. She would have."

"Despite that she is an American."

"Yes, Father." Sebastian looked at Jocelyn and offered a sad smile. "Despite that. Perhaps because of it."

"She is not easily frightened, this one. Even when she doubts herself, she doesn't run away. She faces the problem. By heaven, that's a good quality." He released a groan, sucked in a breath, and continued. "You will need her strength, my son, the way I needed your mother's."

Jocelyn swallowed the thick lump forming in her throat. Were the things the earl said about her true? She wanted them to be true.

"Marry her, Sebastian, with my blessing."

Sebastian leaned close to his father and said, "I *will* marry her, Father. Thank you." He straightened and turned to Jocelyn. "I'll marry her because she's an American and because she is strong and determined and because she isn't easily frightened."

Tears welled in Jocelyn's eyes. Sebastian's image blurred before her.

"I'll marry her for all of those reasons and more." He brushed a strand of hair from the side of her face. "But most of all, I'll marry her because I love her."

Jocelyn sucked in a startled breath. She'd hoped for those words. She'd prayed for those words. But had she believed she would ever hear him say them?

"I suppose that's the only reason that matters, Father. I love her."

She blinked rapidly, wanting to see his face, needing to see his face. She tried to speak, but no sound came from her throat. The best she could do was mouth, *I love you, too.*

"Then, by heaven, boy," his father said, his voice sounding slightly stronger than before, "I intend to be alive and present when you do so. As long as you don't dilly-dally."

Chapter Twenty-Seven

Three days later, Jocelyn stood before the mirror in her bedroom, clad in the summer green dress Mrs. Adler had made for her and wearing a simple straw hat with artificial yellow flowers that Amanda had purchased in Gibeon. Her soon-to-be sister-in-law had helped arrange her hair in the latest fashion. "You are not getting married with your hair in a braid," Amanda had said with a stubborn jut of her chin, and Jocelyn hadn't argued.

Now she smiled at her reflection. Sebastian wouldn't have cared. He liked her hair in a braid. He'd told her so. He'd told her many things as they'd prepared to wed. Mostly that he loved her, but other things too.

Downstairs, voices buzzed as more guests arrived for the wedding of Jocelyn Overstreet of Eden's Gate Ranch, Idaho, to Sebastian Whitcombe, Viscount Willowthorpe, of Hooke Manor, England. For the sake of the Earl of Hooke—who had demanded there be no dilly-dallying—they'd moved the wedding forward in time and changed its location from the church in town to the Overstreet home.

I'm about to marry an English Lord.

She'd tested those words in her heart often over the last few days, waiting to see if the confusion and uncertainty would return. They didn't. Her confidence in the rightness of it only increased. And as her confidence increased, so did her joy. Because she wasn't just marrying an English Lord. She was marrying Sebastian Whitcombe, a man who loved her and who she loved in return.

Not long ago, Amanda had said falling in love was supposed to make a person happier. That hadn't been true of Jocelyn in the beginning. It was true now.

"You've never looked prettier, Miss Joss." Mrs. Adler dabbed at her eyes with a handkerchief.

Jocelyn turned to face the housekeeper and Amanda, both of them wearing their Sunday best.

Amanda said, "It's time. Are you ready?"

"I'm ready."

More than ready. Excited. Filled with anticipation. For today. For the future. For always.

"Son."

Sebastian looked down at his father who sat in a wheelchair. The earl had rallied somewhat over the past couple of days, but he remained too weak to stand as his son spoke his vows. "Yes?"

"May God bless you and Jocelyn, and may He guide you throughout the years to come."

Sebastian felt a pinch in his heart, understanding the words were as close to a goodbye as the earl would likely speak to him. He knew, although no one had spoken of it, that Edward Whitcombe would not set foot in his beloved England again.

"This is not the time for sad thoughts, my boy." His father looked toward the stairs even as a hush fell over the parlor. "Look there. There is your future."

Sebastian turned and watched his bride descend to the ground floor. Amanda and Mrs. Adler followed behind her, both of them smiling and crying. But there were no tears in Jocelyn's eyes. Only love. Love for him.

Her voice came to him from the past. *"Who are you? What are you doing in my brother's house?"*

The memory made him smile. He would never be bored with Jocelyn by his side. He knew it in the depths of his soul. She would challenge him and frustrate him, without a doubt, but she would also bring great joy and laughter into their lives. Most importantly, she would be the helpmeet God had intended for him when He'd brought Sebastian across an ocean and a continent in order to find her, here on Eden's Gate.

Jocelyn reached his side, and he took her hand. Together they faced Reverend Blankenship.

"Dearly beloved . . ."

Their future was about to begin.

If you enjoyed *To Marry an English Lord*, please take a moment to leave a review on Goodreads, BookBub, and/or your favorite retailer.

The British Are Coming.

THE BRITISH ARE COMING series began with *To Enchant a Lady's Heart*, a novella set in Victorian England. It continues with three novels set in America in the mid-1890s featuring Sebastian Whitcombe, heir to the Earl of Hooke; his younger sister, Lady Amanda Whitcombe; and his tradesman friend, Roger Bernhardt. Adventure and romance abound!

TURN THE PAGE FOR A PEEK
AT AMANDA'S STORY
COMING IN WINTER 2024/2025

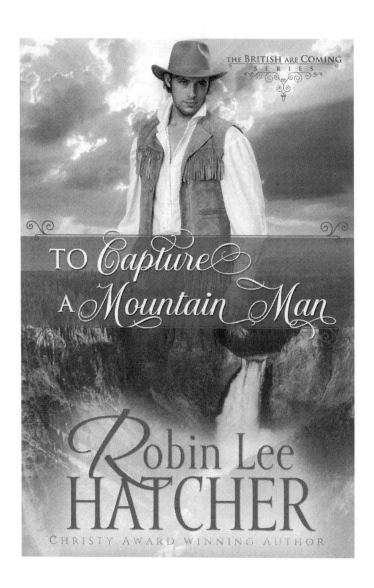

THE BRITISH ARE COMING
SERIES

TO Capture
A Mountain Man

Robin Lee
HATCHER

CHRISTY AWARD WINNING AUTHOR

TO CAPTURE A MOUNTAIN MAN
The British Are Coming, Book 3
Coming Winter 2024/2025
by
Robin Lee Hatcher

Ever since seeing Buffalo Bill's Wild West as a child in London during the Queen's Jubilee, Amanda Whitcombe longed to visit the American West. After several months on Eden's Gate, an Idaho ranch in the shadows of the Grand Tetons, she is more in love with America than she ever imagined. But even she couldn't imagine a man quite like Isaiah Coltrane.

Isaiah wears buckskin clothes, just like Buffalo Bill, but this man is educated and articulate, perhaps even a gentleman. He could live anywhere, do anything, succeed in countless ways, yet he has turned his back on civilization and society.

Isaiah doesn't suffer fools lightly, and if ever he's known foolish women, they come from the titled class in England. And yet Amanda finds a way to capture his carefully guarded heart.

Subscribe to the Robin's Notes to stay informed about new and upcoming releases and sales on her other books.
https://robinleehatcher.com

About the Author

Robin Lee Hatcher is the best-selling author of over 90 books. Her well-drawn characters and heartwarming stories of faith, courage, and love have earned her both critical acclaim and the devotion of readers. Her numerous awards include the Christy Award for Excellence in Christian Fiction, the RITA® Award for Best Inspirational Romance, Romantic Times Career Achievement Awards for Americana Romance and for Inspirational Fiction, the Carol Award, the 2011 Idahope Writer of the Year, and Lifetime Achievement Awards from both Romance Writers of America® (2001) and American Christian Fiction Writers (2014). *Catching Katie* was named one of the Best Books of 2004 by the Library Journal.

When not writing, Robin enjoys being with her family, spending time in the beautiful Idaho outdoors, Bible art journaling, reading books that make her cry, watching romantic movies, knitting, and decorative planning. A mother and grandmother, Robin makes her home on the outskirts of Boise, sharing it with a demanding Papillon dog and a persnickety tuxedo cat.

Learn more about Robin and her books by visiting her website at robinleehatcher.com

You can also find out more by joining her on Facebook, Twitter, or Instagram.

Wagered Heart

The Perfect Life

Speak to Me of Love

Trouble in Paradise

Another Chance to Love You

Bundle of Joy

The British Are Coming

To Enchant a Lady's Heart

To Marry an English Lord

Boulder Creek Romance

Even Forever

All She Ever Dreamed

The Coming to America Series

Dear Lady

Patterns of Love

In His Arms

Promised to Me

Where the Heart Lives Series

Belonging

Betrayal

Beloved

Books set in Kings Meadow

A Promise Kept

Love Without End

Whenever You Come Around

I Hope You Dance

Keeper of the Stars

Books set in Thunder Creek

You'll Think of Me

You're Gonna Love Me

The Sisters of Bethlehem Springs Series

A Vote of Confidence

Fit to Be Tied

A Matter of Character

Legacy of Faith series

Who I am With You

Cross My Heart

How Sweet It Is

For a full list of books, visit robinleehatcher.com

Made in the USA
Middletown, DE
12 February 2024

49561806R00175